SOUL FATED

SHADOW PACK LEGENDS
BOOK TWO

LUNA M. ROSE

BUTTON PRESS

CHAPTER

ONE

CALLISTA

I stared at the lines of code, my eyes darting back and forth as my fingers flew across the keyboard. My home office was a mess, with empty coffee mugs littering the desk and sticky notes plastered haphazardly on the walls. I leaned back, stretching my arms above my head, and glanced at the time.

It was past noon, and I hadn't even bothered to shower. Not that it mattered. I rarely left the house these days. My fingers hovered over the keyboard, and I forced myself to focus. The API integration was almost done, but I still had to optimize the data handling for the client side. Every time I tried to focus, my mind wandered to anything but the task at hand. The JSON responses weren't parsing correctly, and I knew it was just a matter of tweaking the error handling, but the thought of digging through the documentation one more time made my head ache.

I flipped screens to send a quick message to my brother Blake. Evelyn had given me the simplest task known to women—posting about the upcoming bonfire on the pack Discord channel—and I still hadn't done it. They'd been working tirelessly to integrate Kitimat with Black Lake Pack, and I wished I could do more to help. But every time I pushed myself, I ended up collapsing in a heap, unable to function for days.

I pulled up my sleeve and glared down at the bandage covering up the still oozing wound on my arm. As if I suddenly had the ability to will my body to heal.

I hated feeling weak. I hated that Evelyn had gone through so much to protect me, and then here I was giving nothing in return. My wolf whined, dropping her head onto her paws.

You could tell her.

The thought came more frequently these days, but I always shoved it away. It lived with my wolf's desire to stretch her legs and run.

I couldn't let her do it. I didn't know how this wound and the dark magic that caused it would affect her. I was willing to deal with the pain, but I wouldn't risk harming her.

She didn't understand. Or maybe she knew better than I did.

Either way, I fought every day to keep my impulses under control. Ever since that first night when I found myself driving out into the boonies, I had a system. It was called: remain a hermit. So far, ultra successful and also mildly depressing.

I shivered, imagining myself back on that leather couch, looking at Nathan while he explained what he needed from me. At first, I thought he was truly interested in improving himself. In building Kitimat Pack and letting go of his hatred for Rowan and Black Lake. But once I'd overheard his conversation with whoever the hell alpha up north?

It all became clear. He wasn't looking to help Kitimat. He was taking orders from someone who wanted to control us.

That's when I took the dagger. I thought I'd been so smart, taking it home and hiding it in the closet. But now it all made sense. Nathan had been after one more person I loved. He'd lured Evelyn in by leaving the dagger alone, but he hadn't expected Rowan to come with her.

I closed my laptop, and my wound throbbed. I avoided looking at myself as I stood and passed the mirror in the hall. I knew what I looked like. Dark circles ringed my eyes, and my normally wavy hair hung limp around my face. I rubbed my temple, trying to ease the tension that had settled there.

Celeste and Blake were both at work, so I walked into the kitchen and paused at the back glass sliding doors. Outside, the sun shone down on the lush forest, the trees swaying in the breeze. It was beautiful, but it felt like a taunt. I closed my eyes and rested my forehead against the cool glass, my breath fogging the surface.

I needed to find a way to break free of this curse. I couldn't keep living this way. I knew that, but I needed to figure out where to start.

I pushed back and trudged to the fridge. Inside were two containers of leftover chili, a liter of milk, and a tired head of lettuce. Fantastic. Beans made me gassy, and while I loved the idea of lettuce milk, I wanted something a bit more substantial.

I hesitated, doing mental gymnastics to avoid doing what I knew I had to. Blake was working late tonight, and Celeste had been burning the candle on both ends for the past week. I'd found her passed out on the couch more than once, which wasn't like her.

I could do this for them. I could go to the grocery store and get something for dinner, maybe even for the rest of the weekend. I used to love cooking. The thought was almost laughable, considering I'd been living on cheese and crackers or Nutella peanut butter sandwiches for three weeks. And oranges. C'mon, I wasn't a complete heathen.

I slipped on my Vans and walked out the back door, immediately wincing at the brightness of the sun. After holing up for the past few weeks, I half expected my skin to turn to ash.

I walked two blocks, then pushed open the door to our small but mighty Kitimat grocery store, the bell above it chiming to announce my arrival. The faint scent of fresh bread and coffee wafted through the air, and it was almost enough to make me walk to the back corner where I knew I'd find a handful of Elders.

My movements were sluggish, my limbs heavy as I trudged down the narrow aisles. I kept my head down, avoiding eye contact with the few other customers milling about. I passed the shelves lined with canned goods, boxes of cereal, and bags of chips, then turned down the row with the pasta. My phone buzzed in my pocket, and I pulled it out, frowning.

Missed texts and calls. Evelyn's name was at the top, followed by my brother Blake. I swiped them away, my chest tightening. They both worried about me, but what could I say? I was barely holding it together. I shoved the phone back into my pocket, grabbed two boxes of spiral noodles, and tossed them into my basket.

"Callista?"

I turned, my heart skipping a beat. Mrs. Severson, the elderly woman who lived a few houses down from me. Her eyes were kind, but there was a flicker of concern in them that made my stomach churn.

"Afternoon." I forced a tight-lipped smile.

"Callista, dear. You look exhausted." Mrs. Severson's voice was soft, her eyes filled with concern.

My grip tightened on the handle of my basket. "I'm fine. Just tired."

She reached out, her fingers brushing against my arm. "I know you've been through a lot—"

I nodded. "I'm fine, Mrs. Severson."

Her brow furrowed, and she stepped closer, her voice dropping to a whisper. "Bob and I are worried about you, Callista. When your brother told us about your accident—"

"It's just taking some time to get back into the swing of things." I took a step back. My accident. That's what Blake told the mundanes. That I'd gotten in a car accident driving over the pass. It explained why I was gone for a bit and why I looked like absolute shit. I had to give it to him.

Mrs. Severson opened her mouth to say something, but I turned away before she could. I didn't need her pity. I didn't need anyone's pity. I gave a small wave and escaped to the end of the aisle to find tomato sauce.

I couldn't even find solace in these small tasks anymore. Everything felt like a chore, a burden. I longed to be out in the forest, to feel the earth beneath my paws and the wind in my fur. To hunt, to run, to be free. But the idea of shifting made me queasy. This wound wasn't healing for a reason. I'd felt the dark magic in the dagger just by touching the hilt. What if it affected my wolf? What if it got stronger in my shift?

I grabbed zucchini, fresh corn on the cob, and croutons and then headed to the checkout, avoiding the cashier's gaze as I handed over my items.

"I haven't had spaghetti in forever." He scanned the boxes of pasta.

"It's not really..." I trailed off. I didn't have the energy to explain the difference between a ragu and bolognese. I paid for the groceries, grabbed my bag, and pushed open the door, the bell tinkling behind me.

As I stepped onto the sidewalk, the sun was setting, casting a golden glow over the town, but I couldn't enjoy it. I was too aware of the ache in my arm. Too aware of the pull, even now, when I was supposed to be safe inside the borders of our new hybrid Kootenay Pack.

I gritted my teeth and pushed myself back up the hill, then climbed the steps to the house I'd grown up in. I shoved open the door and tossed my bags onto the kitchen counter. I'd only been gone for half an hour, yet my body was so exhausted it felt like I'd been gone for days.

I slumped into a chair and leaned my head against the cool wood of the table. A deep breath calmed my racing heart. A heart that beat too fast. That was my first clue. The pull had been there in the store but weak, like an echo of an echo. Now it was dragging against me in full force. As if the wound were still fresh. As if the dagger were right next to me.

I squeezed my eyes shut and gripped the edge of the table, the wood digging into my fingers. I was stronger than this. I'd been fighting for the last three weeks. I would keep fighting. I wouldn't let it win. Another breath, and I forced myself to my feet, shuffling to the counter to put away the groceries. Once everything was stowed away, I pulled out a pound of ground beef from the freezer and set it in the sink to thaw, then made my way to the washroom. I needed to change the bandages.

I closed the door behind me and locked it, then pulled off my shirt and stared at the wound. I peeled off the bandage, wincing as it pulled at my skin. The wound was open and raw, the edges blackened and cracked. I gritted my teeth and cleaned it as best I could, then applied a fresh bandage. I finished and stood, staring at my reflection in the mirror. My eyes were hollow, my skin pale. I looked like a ghost. Like a shell of the person I'd once been.

I stalked to my bedroom and pulled on a fresh shirt, then went to the kitchen and grabbed a glass of water, my hands shaking. Cooking. I could do cooking.

I turned on my favorite bluegrass group, Arcadian Wild, and pulled a frying pan from the cupboard. The beef wasn't thawed, so I popped it in the microwave for a few minutes on defrost. When I dropped it in the pan, there was still a solid ice core, but at least it was workable.

Though every step seemed to take twice as long as it was supposed to, and I forgot to boil the water for the pasta while I was cooking down the red wine, I eventually ended up with a gorgeous ragu.

I filled a small bowl for myself and covered the rest for Blake and Celeste when they got back, then escaped to my room. I curled onto my bed, burrowed into the pillows, and took my first bite. It was heaven. The savory herbs and smooth sauce made me want to cry.

I glanced at the bottle of sleep aid on the nightstand next to me. This was what I'd been reduced to. Caffeine to keep me up during the day and a pill to force my head to go quiet. I'd tried everything I could think of. Meditation, herbal remedies, even acupuncture. Nothing worked. The pain was always there, a constant throbbing that never let up. And the dreams. The dreams were the worst.

I finished my food, took a drink from my water bottle, and changed into a tank top and sweats. I swiped a make-up wipe over my face and reached for the bottle. I took a deep breath and swallowed the pill, then climbed into bed, pulling the comforter over my shoulders.

The pain was always worse at night, but after fifteen minutes, when the drug took effect, everything disappeared for eight to ten hours. It was glorious. I'd tried taking the pill earlier to avoid the pain, but then I woke up before the sun rose. Not worth it for my day to be longer.

The ache in my arm started as a dull throb, then grew sharper, more insistent. I squeezed my eyes shut, trying to block it out. It was like a knife twisting in my side, tearing through flesh and muscle.

And then there were the images.

A shadow loomed in front of me, its edges blurred and indistinct. My thoughts scattered like leaves in the wind, disjointed and fragmented. I clutched my side, my fingers digging into the fabric of my shirt. The wound burned, a searing heat that radiated through my body. I gritted my teeth, a bead of sweat rolling down my temple.

Ten more minutes. I tried to force my eyes open, but they stayed closed, heavy as lead. Panic clawed at my throat. I was trapped, caught between the waking world and the dream, unable to escape.

The shadow grew darker, its edges sharpening until the dagger lay on the grass in front of me. It pulsed with a sinister energy. I tried to pull away, but my hand wouldn't obey. I watched in horror as my fingers closed over the hilt, the blade glowing a sickly green, the runes etched into the metal writhing like snakes.

This wasn't real.

I took a deep breath and tried to push the dagger away, to banish it from my mind. But it was no use. It was like trying to move a mountain with my bare hands. The light grew brighter, and I cried out, my back arching. The pain was unbearable, like molten lava coursing through my veins. I clamped my mouth shut, refusing to scream. I wouldn't give it the satisfaction.

You can't control me. The words echoed in my head, a

desperate mantra. I repeated them, trying to drown out the voice that whispered in my ear.

You are mine.

I shook my head, my vision blurring. It wasn't real. It couldn't be real—

Light suddenly erupted in front of me, and an image of a clearing in the woods appeared. Even in my feverish state, I could smell the sharp tang of pine and hear the whisper of the wind through the branches. It was a place of peace and beauty, a place I knew well. Cotton Creek Campground. I'd recognize that wooden bridge anywhere.

My mind transported me back to my childhood, to the feeling of the sun on my skin and birds chirping in the trees. I could see the giant tree I used to climb, its gnarled branches stretching like arms. Or the brook where I used to catch frogs, its water clear and cool.

But as I focused on the memory, there was a shift. The sun disappeared behind a cloud, and the air grew colder. The creek's water turned murky, and the shadows lengthened. The redwoods swayed in the wind, their branches creaking like old bones.

I scanned the clearing, my eyes searching for any sign of movement, but there was nothing. Just the trees and the water and the shadows. I wanted to run, to turn and flee, but my feet were rooted to the ground.

And then the darkness closed in, and I began slipping away. The trees and the creek faded as I sank into the mattress.

Finally. I fell into a deep, dreamless sleep.

CHAPTER
TWO

KAEL

I found a secluded spot deep in the woods to pull off the main road, far from the main camping area. The last thing I wanted was to be disturbed, plus I preferred the quiet of the wilderness anyway. I'd been living among humans long enough to know the difference between those who were dangerous and those who were not. The people who frequented this place were the type found near the lake, dipping their toes in the water or telling stories around a campfire.

Still. It made me nervous to be surrounded. People always had questions when they saw me, especially kids. They got one look at my rolled up left sleeve and couldn't help but point. Ask if I got in an accident or something and then give me a pitying look.

The truth was, I'd never known life with two fully functioning arms. I was perfectly capable with one and a half. I was always tempted to show them, but I doubted that dropping their dad to the ground in a headlock would make the right first impression.

I made them just as nervous as they made me. I'd learned young that it was better to keep to myself.

This section of the forest was lush and green, the opposite of where I'd been over the last year. The air was fresh, and I took a deep breath as my hiking boots crunched against the forest floor. This was a place I could almost feel at peace.

When I reached a break in the trees, I stopped and sighed, rolling my shoulders to relieve the tension of carrying my pack. I needed to stay sharp, but I had to rest. I could go for several days before my body started to break down, but that was if I was only traveling. As Nathan Black had already proved with this assignment, I needed to be ready for anything.

I dropped my pack from my shoulders and laid it out on the ground, then popped up my backpacking tent and unfurled my sleeping mat. Once everything was in place, I sat on the soft earth and leaned back against a tree trunk, closing my eyes for a moment. The coolness of the bark seeped through my shirt, grounding me.

It was strange being in pack territory again. I'd spent so long avoiding it, the scents put me off balance. I gave my wolf plenty of time to run free, but he was used to being alone. Flying solo. It was understandable that he was conflicted about this change in setting.

Flashes of anger, grief, and confusion had been hitting me all week. Ever since the Alliance had sent me into Black Lake. I was young enough that I didn't remember the details of what had happened the night my mother left me in the woods, but my wolf did. He remembered everything.

I, on the other hand, considered it a favor. I learned how to survive a hell of a lot faster than I would've had I been coddled in a pack. I had always been able to mask my scent, but it was a skill I had honed out of necessity. When I was young, I learned to hide in the undergrowth. I learned to move silently, to blend into the shadows. I convinced myself it was only a game I was playing, not life and death.

I let out a long breath. Ironic that now I dealt in life and death for living.

I was perfect for it. I had no ties, no lingering attachments to my past. I'd lost track of my mother years prior, and I had no siblings I knew about. No mate. Wolves like Nathan Black proved that it took a special kind of bastard to handle the dagger. He cared too much. About himself, about power, and apparently about a she-wolf that must have given damn good tail to inspire that kind of vengeance.

The Alliance needed someone with a cold, dead heart, and they'd found it in me. Not as cold as I would've liked since I was only doing this for Destin. There were very few wolves I'd be willing to kill for, but he was one of them.

I pushed up from the ground and pulled two sticks of beef jerky, an apple, and three pieces of bread from my pack. Dinner of champions.

It wouldn't be long before I was back on a plane to Europe or Africa, or wherever the next contract took me. There was a never ending wait list, and I'd lived on every continent, learning the languages and cultures.

All I needed to do was complete the task Nathan had been given. I'd been hired the second that asshole started to go rogue, and if the Black Lake alpha wouldn't have ripped out his throat, I sure as hell would've.

I'd been given the instructions as Nathan had. Five shifters, one from every pack in the province. The blood had to be spilled on the dagger, and then the Alliance could take the next step. I didn't know what that was specifically, but I knew what they were after. Control. Power. The dagger would consolidate their control in British Columbia. The packs would be forced under their rule.

It would've been a simple task had the asshat Nathan Black not used the dagger to get his jollies. None of the alphas fully understood the magic held in the relic, but they knew that once it tasted blood, it needed all of it. Needed to take the life of the owner. I didn't want to know how they figured that out.

But the second I'd tried to drive east, the dagger had flared to life, hitting me with a pull so strong I nearly swerved off the road.

Now my task wasn't so cut and dry. I was taking orders from a damn piece of metal.

I finished my meal and shoved my trash into the plastic bag in my pack, then pulled out my sidearm, checking the chamber and magazine. I loaded an extra mag into my belt pouch and threw my bag onto the back seat of my truck.

One more leg tomorrow, one more night in the woods, and then I'd be back to where I started three weeks ago. It wasn't a surprise that the dagger was leading me straight back to Kitimat and Black Lake territory. The only piece left to put in place was where the dagger would lead me once I got there.

CHAPTER

THREE

Callista

I woke with a start, an oppressive weight on my chest. I kicked off the covers, gasping for air, drenched in sweat.

Why was I seeing that damn campground? I wasn't normally a dreamer, but every since the dagger touched my skin, my mind seemed to come alive at night. The campground was a family favorite, one I went to for years with my family and Evelyn's. There were only happy memories there. I found it hard to believe the dagger was searching for those in my psyche.

My legs shook as I swung them over the edge of my bed, every muscle weak and trembling. I made it to the washroom and splashed water on my face, but it didn't improve the palor of my skin. I looked like a ghost.

My arm throbbed, and there wasn't even a question of whether I was going to make it to breakfast with Evelyn and

14

the others. I reached for my phone. My fingers fumbled as I punched out a quick text.

Not feeling well. Catch you next weekend

I SET the phone on the counter, then wrapped my fingers around the edge of the sink and took a deep breath.

It was Friday. I had the weekend to get myself together and be ready for work Monday morning. I probably had time to take a little side quest...

I squeezed my eyes shut and clenched my fists just as I did every day. *No.* I couldn't follow this pull. I couldn't give in to whatever dark magic the dagger had embedded in my skin.

But something was different today. It didn't work. My body wasn't listening. I felt like I was floating above my head as I pushed off the counter and padded into the kitchen. It was early, but if I was going to do this, I had to get on the road. *Stop! I couldn't do this!*

I opened the cupboard and pulled out a package of protein bars and a bag of trail mix I'd picked up for my last hike, then grabbed my electric kettle and a box of tea bags before heading to my closet.

My camping gear was stashed in the back. I pulled out my pack and started tossing in clothes. I didn't need much. I was only planning to stay a couple of nights. And probably die a gruesome death, at which point, nobody would care if my underwear was clean, amiright?

I couldn't even make myself chuckle. I grabbed a flashlight, my sleeping bag, and a small pillow, then zipped up my bag, my hands trembling.

I glanced around my apartment. *What else did I need?* I wasn't planning on hiking far, but I didn't know what to expect. A first-aid kit would be smart. I shoved that and my toothbrush plus deodorant into the top pocket of my pack, then slung it over my shoulder and made my way to the door.

A picture frame teetered on the edge of the console in the entry as I slid into my hiking boots. I caught it just before it fell, then turned it over and set it down on the table. I didn't want to see Blake and Celeste's smiling faces. Not now.

My bag was heavy as I shrugged it onto my back and fumbled with the zipper on my jacket. The days were getting warmer, but there was still a chill in the air in the mornings.

My heart leaped into my throat as someone knocked on the door. I glanced at my phone. There was no message from Blake or Celeste, and I wasn't expecting anyone.

I took a deep breath, trying to calm my racing heart, as the knock came again, and I forced myself to stand. I approached the door, my hands trembling as I reached for the handle. I opened it slowly, my eyes widening as I took in Evelyn. Standing on my doorstep. Hadn't I told her I wasn't available?

I let out a slow breath, then threw my pack next to the couch and opened the door. "Hey, I thought you were supposed to be at the cafe." I tried to give Evelyn a quick hug, but she wrapped her arms around me and wouldn't let me go.

"Why do you have a jacket on if you're sick?" Evelyn pulled back and cupped my cheeks, her green eyes searching mine. Her auburn hair cascaded over one shoulder, and she wore a simple tunic and leggings

"I was...cold."

Evelyn looked down at the floor. "You needed your hiking boots?"

"Evelyn—"

"You were ditching breakfast to go hiking? With who?" Her nostrils flared as she dropped her hands.

"With myself, and I wasn't ditching breakfast, I just—"

"Nobody gets up at the butt-crack of dawn on a Friday if they don't have to. What's going on, Calli?" Her eyes bored into mine.

I wasn't going to get away with a half-assed excuse this time. "There's something I need to do."

"Great. Why don't we do it together? We could do it on the way." Evelyn turned back to the driveway.

"On the way to wha..." That's when I noticed Rowan in the truck. He opened the driver's side door and stepped out onto the driveway.

"Hey, Callista." Rowan waved and started toward the stairs.

"You brought the alpha?" I hissed, and Evelyn raised a brow.

"Desperate times."

I scoffed. "This isn't desperate. Just because I'm not coming to breakfast—"

"You haven't been to anything, Callista. I came this morning to make sure someone hadn't stolen your phone after murdering you and burying you in the basement!" Evelyn saw the expression on my face and pursed her lips. "Sorry. Way too soon for hyperbole."

It *was* too soon. Three weeks ago, I was convinced that would be my fate. My heart softened at the realization that Evelyn and Rowan were why I stood on my porch. My life was a dumpster fire, but at least I still had it.

She leaned against the doorframe with a smirk on her lips, tucking her auburn hair behind her ear. Rowan walked up the steps and stood behind her.

"We have a surprise for you." Evelyn's voice was chipper.

I swallowed hard, my mind still sluggish after my dream and forced a smile. If I could play along, maybe they'd go away faster. "What kind of surprise?"

Rowan's smile widened, and he exchanged a glance with Evelyn. "We're going camping. Just for the night. We thought getting away and enjoying the fresh air would be fun."

My heart dropped to my knees. *Was I still dreaming?* I opened my mouth to protest, but the words caught in my throat. I couldn't tell them about the dagger or the dark magic. I couldn't tell them I had other plans. They'd know I was lying.

"I... I don't know if that's a good idea," I stammered, my voice trembling. "I haven't been sleeping well."

Evelyn frowned. "Why not?"

I shrugged, taking a step back in the entryway. "Just bad dreams."

Evelyn nodded. "I know exactly what you mean. Those images...I can't get them out of my head either."

I gritted my teeth. Of course. Evelyn had been in the clearing with Nathan, too. Since she was functional, I should be functional. She'd gone through just as much as I had. "I don't have a good feeling about leaving the house."

Evelyn winced. "Callista, you can't hole up here forever."

I pulled my sleeve lower over my wrist. "It's not forever."

"It feels like it." She met my eyes, and I knew she wouldn't leave my porch with a little pushback like she had in the past.

"Where do you want to go?"

Evelyn grinned. "Site 406. At Cotton Creek. Where we used to camp as kids."

My stomach turned inside out. "Evelyn—"

"You haven't been in forever, I asked Blake." She pushed out her lower lip. "It'll be fun, Calli. Like old times."

She was trying so hard. It was heartbreaking. But the image from my dream flared with disturbing detail. It was the same place. How was it possible that I'd seen the park in my dreams, and now they were standing here trying to convince me to go there?

Rowan put a protective arm around her waist. "Jasper and I will both be there."

I shook my head, my heart pounding in my chest. "I can't."

Evelyn crossed her arms over her chest and stared at me. "Callista, you agreed to let us help you. And now you're refusing to listen to our advice. You have to trust us."

"I do trust you," I whispered, my voice breaking. "But this is—"

"Lana will be here to pick you up at four. Be ready." Evelyn stared at me, unblinking, daring me to argue. She glanced down at my bag on the floor behind me. "Oddly, it seems like you might already be prepped for this."

I opened my mouth, but the words fizzled on my tongue. Evelyn stepped inside and hugged me again, then turned and walked away with Rowan, leaving me standing in the doorway with my heart racing and my mind spinning.

I slammed the door shut and leaned against it, my chest heaving with shallow breaths. I collapsed onto the floor, pressing my back against the cool wood. My body trembled, and my breaths came in short, ragged gasps.

I closed my eyes, trying to steady my racing heart. How had I gotten here? How had I let myself become so isolated? I thought back to all the times I'd canceled plans, made excuses, retreated into my own world. I'd cried wolf too many times.

I clenched my fists, my nails digging into my palms. I couldn't blame Evelyn and Rowan for not understanding. They didn't know the terror that gripped me every night, the darkness that whispered in my ear.

They didn't know about the dream.

I shuddered, the memory of it flashing before my eyes. The forest. The shadows.

My breath hitched, and I forced myself to open my eyes. The sun streamed through the windows, casting dappled patterns on the floor. The house was silent, the only sound the ticking of the clock on the mantel. I glanced up. Ten thirty-two.

I pressed my hand to my arm, feeling the bandage beneath my shirt. The wound no longer ached as it had in my bedroom. It felt... satisfied. Like it knew it was getting what it wanted. I shivered, my skin prickling with unease.

I pushed myself to my feet, my legs shaky. I wasn't getting out of this. The only way I'd get far enough away to avoid Evelyn or Lana finding me was if I got in my truck, and that wasn't an option. Or...I could tell her.

Also not an option.

I walked to the kitchen and grabbed a cloth, wetting it under the faucet. I scrubbed. I loaded the dishwasher. I used a toothbrush on the sink.

Once I finished cleaning the kitchen, I moved on to the living room, dusting the shelves and vacuuming the rug. The house was spotless by the time I was done, but the knot of anxiety in my stomach hadn't loosened.

I grabbed my hiking backpack and double-checked that I had a change of clothes, a water bottle, some snacks, and toiletries. *Only one night.* I felt like I'd strapped in on a roller coaster, and the ride was about to start. Maybe there was a reason I was supposed to go there. Maybe the dream wasn't from the shadows...maybe it was from my wolf? Maybe she was trying to tell me something? Trying to help me heal?

I set the bag back by the door and pulled out my laptop. I had to find something to occupy my mind. I searched relics, occult dangers, dark magic, and daggers like I had a thousand times before, hoping for anything I could sink my teeth into.

The results were the same as they had been the last time I'd searched. Legends of cursed blades and stories of ancient rituals. I skimmed the pages, my frustration growing. I needed something concrete. Something that would help me understand what I was dealing with.

Instead, I found different versions of the stories we'd heard as kids about powerful packs and cursed alphas. I scrolled... and scrolled and scrolled, stopping briefly on one blog post called *The Shadow Pack: Legends of British Columbia* that at least had some gorgeous images of the coast. I clicked on the link, my eyes scanning the text.

THE SHADOW PACK was tasked with protecting the shifters that guarded the veil between the living world and the Shadow Realm, a place where souls lingered, and dark magic thrived. They were entrusted with the knowledge of ancient rituals that could either protect the world from the forces of darkness or unleash them upon—

I JUMPED, sending my laptop to the rug as a fist pounded on the door, and I glanced at the clock. *Four.* My blood ran cold.

"Just a second!" I hastily scribbled a note for Blake and Celeste, grabbed my gear, and opened the door.

Lana stood there, her expression unreadable."Ready?" She wore a fitted black leather jacket and pants.

I crossed my arms over my chest, my skin prickling. "I don't need a babysitter." Especially one that looked like Lara Croft.

Lana raised an eyebrow, a smirk playing at the corner of her lips. "Good. Because I'm shit at changing diapers."

CHAPTER

FOUR

Kael

It didn't look like much from the outside, but I'd been on the road long enough to know not to judge a gas station by its peeling paint and questionable signage. It was all about the selection of energy drinks. I needed high caffeine and a lot of it. With my wolf metabolism, six energy drinks was the bare minimum for a two-hour drive.

I pulled up to the pump and unscrewed my gas cap, the smell of gasoline mixing with the crisp northern air. The nozzle clicked as I started to fill the tank, and I glanced around, taking in the scene.

The corner store sat like an old sentinel, its wooden slats weathered from years of exposure to the elements. The sign above the door creaked in the wind, announcing its presence as "Marty's General Store." I finished filling the tank, then walked across the gravel lot and pushed open the door. A bell

22

jingled overhead, and I stepped inside, the warmth of the store wrapping around me like a familiar blanket.

The place was a throwback to a simpler time. Rustic wooden shelves lined the walls, filled with a haphazard mix of essentials and local oddities. There were jars of honey with handwritten labels, chunks of soap that looked like they'd been carved from a block, and a display of beaded necklaces that I couldn't imagine anyone wearing.

I scanned the shelves, my eyes landing on the more practical items. Canned food, batteries, a small first aid kit. I grabbed a few cans of beans and soup, then added my drinks, they had Uptime which was a plus, and a pack of trail mix to my basket. It was embarrassing to think about how many years I'd stayed alive on crap like this.

As I approached the counter, my boots scuffed against the cracked linoleum. The cashier, a wiry man with a bushy mustache, nodded in acknowledgment as he rang up my items and put them in a plastic bag.

The bell above the door jingled again, and I glanced up. A mom with two kids entered, but my eyes were drawn like magnets to the back of a woman's head bobbing down the aisle, her long hair catching the light from the window.

My heart seemed to skip a beat, and the dagger's energy flared inside me. *What the hell?* I stepped forward, snagging my bag from the counter, my eyes still glued to her. She pushed the door forward and stepped out into the sunlight.

I rushed outside to the sidewalk, watching her walk to a truck parked at the pump. Something about the way she moved, the way her hair fell over her shoulder, made everything inside me shift.

I stood there, frozen, as she climbed into the passenger seat and slammed the door. It wasn't until the engine roared to life and the truck started to pull away from the pump that I snapped back to reality.

The truck pulled out onto the highway, and I didn't even notice the man at the counter speaking until he raised his voice. "Hey, you planning to pay for those?"

I blinked, the spell breaking. What the hell had just happened? My heart still pounded in my chest, and I glanced down at the dagger, running my fingertips over the hilt. It was warm to the touch, as if it had come to life.

"Sir?" The cashier raised a brow. "I can't just let you walk out with those."

I nodded, reaching into my pocket. "Right. Sorry." I pulled out my wallet and handed him a twenty. "Keep the change."

He took the bill, his eyes narrowing suspiciously. "You okay there, bud? Looked like you'd seen a ghost."

The last thing I wanted to have a conversation with a stranger about was seeing the back of a woman's head and losing my shit. "I'm fine. Just tired, I guess." I grabbed my groceries and walked out the door, not giving him a chance to respond.

As I returned to the truck, I couldn't shake the feeling that something within me had knocked off its axis. The way the dagger had responded to that woman. No, it had responded to her leaving. I shoved the cans into the cab and climbed in, not bothering to close the door. The engine roared to life, and I pulled out onto the highway, turning in the same direction the truck had gone. South.

I gripped the steering wheel, my knuckles turning white. What had I just done? I didn't even know where she was going, and there were a million places she could turn off before I caught up to her.

My mind raced as I thought back to the dagger. It had been warm. Alive. It had been cold in the parking lot. Cold in my hotel room. Cold the entire time I'd been up north looking for the Shadow Pack and the relics.

But the moment I saw her, the moment she stepped out of the store, it had started to burn. I thought about the prophecy. The relics that had been created by Seraphina and the Shadow Pack.

The dagger was one of them. I knew that. I'd seen it in the illustrations.

But why? Why had it reacted to that woman?

I gripped the steering wheel as my eyes scanned the road ahead. I was almost to the edge of the town, and I hadn't caught a glimpse of their truck. My heart sank, but I kept driving, hoping I'd see them at the next turnoff.

I didn't.

I swore under my breath, pulled off at the next exit, and turned around. The dagger pulsed at my side like it was mocking me.

"What do you want?" I growled, but the blade didn't answer.

I followed the highway back into town, my eyes scanning the road. The buildings. The parking lots. I didn't know what I was looking for, but I knew something was there—

The dagger flared, and I slammed on the brakes. My truck skidded to a stop on the shoulder, and I pushed it into park. The blade hummed at my side, and I closed my eyes, trying to focus.

It could sense something. *I* could sense something. The dagger was like a compass, pointing me south. I didn't know what I'd find, but I had to follow it.

FIVE

Callista

The truck engine hummed beneath me as we pulled out of the gas station parking lot, and I shifted in the passenger seat, crossing my arms over my chest. Tall evergreens blurred past the window, their dark limbs stretching toward the sky, and I resisted the urge to drum my fingers on the armrest. I wanted to play music, but Lana didn't seem like the chill, folksy type and that was everything on my playlist as of late.

Lana gripped the steering wheel. The muscles in her forearms flexed as she navigated another curve in the road. I glanced at the speedometer.

"Do you have a problem with my driving, Callista?" Her eyes were trained on the road ahead.

I shook my head. "Zero problems." I didn't trust myself to drive, and I was glad she didn't question it.

It was a three-hour drive, and we were making good time. We'd only had to stop once for gas and food. The donair I'd picked up at the gas station had left much to be desired, but at least it hadn't given me food poisoning.

"Almost there," Lana murmured, her voice softer now. I glanced at her, catching the flicker of something in her eyes before she turned her attention back to the road.

I nodded, swallowing the lump in my throat. "Yeah." There was a time, not so long ago, when I would've been thrilled at the idea of a road trip through the woods. Evelyn and I used to pack the car full of camping gear and snacks, our suitcases stuffed, and head out on our next adventure. Now? I was terrified.

My thoughts drifted to the camping trip Evelyn and I took one summer as kids. We were both nine or ten, and Evelyn had insisted on packing the car herself, refusing to let our parents help. She'd stuffed the backseat with pillows and blankets, creating a nest for us to curl up in during the drive.

I could still smell the sun-warmed leather of her family's old Subaru, hear the way she'd sung along to the radio, her voice always a half-step behind, and see how her eyes crinkled at the corners when she glanced back at me. She'd taught me how to roast marshmallows to the perfect golden brown, and we'd stayed up late, whispering secrets under the stars.

I clenched my teeth at the memory, a bitter taste coating my tongue. This wasn't a camping trip with s'mores and blanket nests.

Lana glanced at me, her eyes narrowing. "You're staring again."

I huffed out a breath and turned my gaze to the trees. The blur of green felt like it was swallowing me whole. I could almost feel the forest closing in, pressing against the windows, threatening to suffocate me.

These last forty minutes were going to be torture if we couldn't find some way to pass the time. "So. Evelyn tells me you're a teacher?"

Lana nodded. "Yep. Special Ed. I start back at the end of August."

"Why did you choose that?" I asked, my curiosity getting the better of me. She didn't seem like the warm and fuzzy type.

Lana's eyes flicked to the rearview mirror, then back to the road. "My brother." Her voice softened, and I could see the muscles in her jaw relax slightly. "He had muscular dystrophy. He was my best friend."

Was. I sucked in a breath, my heart squeezing at the raw emotion in her voice. "I'm sorry."

Lana shrugged, her shoulders tight. "It was a long time ago. But it's why I do what I do. Teaching helped me cope. It gave me a purpose." Her gaze flicked to me, then back to the road. "Rowan was there for me. For my family. It's not something I'll ever forget."

I cleared my throat. "Tell me more about him. About the pack." I'd been gobsmacked to find out that not only was Evelyn back, but she was fated to Rowan Steele. The stories I heard about him weren't good, but I'd always taken them with a grain of salt. Everyone in Kitimat knew how Nathan felt about Black Lake's alpha. Now that I had first-hand experience seeing how deeply Nathan had entrenched himself with the alphas in the north and, apparently, dark magic, I wondered if I needed to rewrite my version of history.

"Rowan's a good man. Kind."

That was true. I remembered him as a kid. Evelyn had been better friends with him than I was, and...I realized right then that my bias against Rowan had started at fourteen. The day I found out Evelyn had gone with him to the creek instead of calling me. Was I jealous of him? No. That was ridiculous. I was happy for my friend, wasn't I?

Lana clicked her tongue. "I was proud that Rowan took his place as alpha. The whole thing...it was a mess."

I remembered. It had been years, but we were still too close to the day our pack split. It felt like we were being yo-yo'd with it joining back together. "I think it will be good. Especially with everything going on. We need to band together."

I said it like we had a tough work schedule or something. Not that dark magic was working to infiltrate our towns and our lives. Even after seeing Nathan with the dagger, I still didn't know what he wanted. Why was he working with the alphas in the north? Why did he come back looking for blood? He wanted Evelyn, but I doubted the alphas had given him a powerful ancient relic to force his ex back into his arms.

He'd killed with that dagger. He'd wanted to kill me.

I shivered as the car rounded a bend, and I caught a glimpse of a lake through the trees. My heart skipped a beat, and I leaned forward, straining to see.

"Really almost there," Lana said, her voice breaking through my thoughts.

I nodded, my pulse quickening. I barely noticed the growing throb in my arm. I had no idea what we were walking into, but we couldn't turn back now.

The car crested a hill, and the lake came into view, the water shimmering in the fading light. I held my breath, my eyes scanning the shore. There. A cluster of tents and cars. People milling about, setting up camp.

We followed the path toward the campsite, and I immediately caught the scent of roasting hot dogs. My stomach growled in response. I hadn't eaten since breakfast.

Lana and I stepped into the clearing, and I stopped in my tracks, taking in the scene. At least fifteen pack members were there, bustling around, setting up tents and campfires. The air was filled with laughter and the clatter of camping gear, the sounds bouncing off the towering redwoods surrounding us.

I spotted Rowan and Evelyn right away. Rowan was talking to Will and Marissa, who I recognized from the week before. Her pregnant belly looked like it was about to burst. Evelyn was chatting animatedly with a couple I didn't know. Probably more of the Black Lake pack. I scanned the crowd, noting Finn, the doctor who had initially looked at my arm, and Jasper standing near a cooler.

As I watched, a couple of kids ran past, giggling as they chased each other around the campsite. My heart warmed at the sight. What would it be like to run like that, so carefree? To not be constantly thinking about pain?

Rowan spotted us first. He nudged Evelyn, and they walked over, leaving their conversations mid-sentence.

"Callista, Lana, glad you could make it." Rowan grinned.

Because I definitely had a choice.

"Isn't it great out here? I swear the trees are bigger." Evelyn sucked in a lungful of air.

I nodded. "Gorgeous." Truthfully, I'd barely looked around. Everything that used to bring me joy seemed frayed at the edges.

Evelyn pointed at the bag in Lana's arms. "Do you need help setting up your tent?"

Lana shook her head. "I think we've got it."

Not once had I thought about the fact that I'd be sharing a tent with Lana. Not that it made any sense to share with Evelyn now that she was with Rowan, but because I'd never corrected the image in my head, the one with me and her together was still there.

"Alright, well, let us know if you need anything. We

brought extra sleeping bags and blankets, just in case." Rowan turned to me, assessing.

"Thanks." I dropped my eyes.

They walked back to their friends, and I followed Lana to an open patch of grass. "I'm sure they've bribed you with something good to babysit me for the night, but you don't need to do this. We could just go home."

Lana laughed. "Yeah. That's not happening."

Before I could argue, Maya approached us with a warm smile. "Hey, Callista! Lana! It's so great to see you here." She was petite, with curly brown hair and bright blue eyes. *What was I, the community project?*

Maya's family had camped with us on a few occasions, but she was so much younger than Evelyn and me, I hadn't paid her much attention.

Lana gave her a quick smile before dumping out the contents of our tent bag. "Just getting settled."

Maya smiled. "Callista, remember when we all had that midnight snack raid on the cooler?"

My brows pinched, but then I remembered what she was talking about. "Blake just about murdered me when he found out we ate all the s'mores ingredients."

"It was mostly us little kids. You guys took the brunt of the punishment."

That was true. My parents had forced us on a murderous hike the next morning.

Maya chuckled, her eyes sparkling. "It's funny. I never thought I'd miss camping, but here I am, nostalgic as hell."

She gave a small wave and jogged back to her side of the camp. Lana and I finished setting up the tent and rolled out our sleeping bags, then wandered toward the food.

". . . and if you think about it, the hot dog is essentially the perfect encapsulation of modern food engineering. It's convenient, high in protein, and—" Finn adjusted his glasses. "—has a decent amount of sodium, which, while not ideal for daily consumption, can be beneficial when we're exerting a lot of energy."

"Here we go." Lana rolled her eyes as we approached Rowan, Finn, and Jasper.

Jasper stared at him, his expression deadpan. "Finn, you could make a sandwich out of drywall sound appealing."

Finn shrugged. "I'm just saying they're underrated. Nutritionally speaking."

Jasper snorted. "Right, because when I think of nutrition, I think of processed meat tubes."

Finn held up a finger. "Actually, if you look at the ingredients—"

"Please don't." Jasper held up a hand. "I don't need a dissertation on the culinary merits of hot dogs. Let me enjoy my trash food." He grabbed a beer out of the cooler and handed one to Finn.

Rowan appeared from behind the tent, his eyebrows raised. "What are we talking about?"

Jasper leaned against a tree. "Finn was going off on how sausages are misunderstood."

"I think your sausage has been very clear about its intentions," Lana quipped, and I almost laughed out loud.

How long had it been since I laughed? My arm was so calm, I hadn't thought about it since we pulled up. Strange.

Jasper grinned. "Consistent marketing. That's my mantra."

"Hungry?" Finn offered Lana and Callista a paper plate, then pointed them toward the table with buns, condiments, and extras.

I looked at the spread. "I should've brought something."

Rowan shook his head. "Nope. This was extra from the long weekend. Needed to be used up."

I made up a hot dog and had just dipped the spoon in the potato salad when Blake and Celeste walked up. They both grinned when they spotted me, and Blake strode over, pulling me into a tight hug, nearly spilling the food on my plate. "Hey, Sis."

"Hey. Took you long enough." I returned to scooping salad. He didn't have to say anything for me to know what he was thinking. *How did they finally get you to crawl out of your shell?*

Blake laughed. "Some of us had to work."

"Okay, ouch."

Celeste rolled her eyes. "He's kidding. By the way, we would've been way later if you hadn't taken care of things at home."

I nodded, my throat tight. "I'm just glad you could both get away. I know it's been a lot lately."

Blake nodded, understanding passing between us. "We also convinced a few other Kitimat pack members to join. We thought it would be good for morale." He gestured behind him, and I noticed a couple of familiar faces unloading gear from another vehicle.

"That's great. The more the merrier." I glanced around the campsite, noting the smiles and nods from our pack members as Celeste and Blake greeted them. This was good. We needed more people from our neck of the woods integrated with Black Lake.

The sun lowered over the peaks behind us, and the campsite lit up in gold. It did look different than I remembered. Both bigger and smaller. The last time I'd been there my world had been the size of Kitimat and surrounding area. Everything had seemed new and fresh, and now it looked a little tired. It wasn't that I was a world traveler, but I'd taken enough trips to make it seem like my town had shrunk.

We finished our food, and I helped clean up with the

others, then sat on a camp chair Lana brought around the fire Jasper had made. By the size of the blaze, he was planning to sit there for the next three hours.

Rowan stood by the fire, his piercing blue eyes reflecting the dying light. The flickering flames cast shadows on his face, making him appear even more commanding. He raised a hand, and the ambient noise slowly died down.

The crackling of the fire became the only sound, its warmth brushing over my skin. I understood how Rowan had drawn Evelyn in. He was magnetic. Definitely not the same boy we'd known growing up. But that was the alpha in him, wasn't it? Or had that strength always been there, and we hadn't been looking for it?

My dad always used to say, 'Alphas aren't born. They're made.' Most shifters believed there was something in their genetic code that made alphas, and it was only a matter of time before they presented. But not him. He believed they were born out of necessity. That many were capable, but only a few chose to step into that role. He had so much faith in alphas. I wondered what he would've said about Nathan Black after he'd singlehandedly dragged our pack through the mud.

"Thank you all for coming," Rowan began. "This has been a difficult time for our pack, for all of us. But seeing you all here standing together, it reminds me of our strength. Our unity."

Evelyn sat beside him, her hand resting on his arm as she leaned toward him in her chair. I wanted to be happy for my friend. I *was* happy for her. That happiness was just buried under something I couldn't quite put my finger on. Jealousy, yes. But not because I wanted someone like Rowan or even that I wanted a relationship. I just wanted...things to go back to normal. I wanted my life before Evelyn left Kitimat. Before Nathan Black lost his sanity.

But it was ridiculous to keep wishing for something that

couldn't happen. I'd survived without Evelyn before, and I could do it again. It just sucked that we didn't have some time to figure ourselves out before she mated. Wasn't that what Evelyn was trying to do? Spend time with me? I was the problem now, always pushing back.

"We've faced challenges," Rowan continued. "And we've lost . . . good people." His voice caught, and Evelyn squeezed his arm.

My heart twinged at the thought of the still missing wolves. We knew Nathan was responsible for at least one death but had no trace on the others.

Finn sat on Rowan's right while Jasper poked at the red-hot coals. Blake and Celeste stood at the back, their silhouettes dark against the fading light.

Rowan's gaze swept over the group, landing on each of us in turn. A shiver ran down my spine when his eyes met mine. "I know there are still questions. Things we don't understand." His voice was steady, but I could hear the undercurrent of frustration. "But we will find answers. We will protect our pack. And we will honor those we've lost by standing together, stronger than ever."

The fire crackled, sending a shower of sparks into the air. Rowan's eyes lingered on me for a moment longer before he looked away. My chest tightened with a surge of emotion. I wanted to believe him, to trust that we could overcome whatever lay ahead. But the shadows of doubt were hard to dispel, especially because the evidence of it was burrowed deep in my arm.

I was far enough back from the fire, I hoped no one besides Lana would notice me leaving the fire ring. I pushed up from my chair and walked into the woods. I should've predicted Evelyn's hawk-like attention since she hadn't stopped watching me since I'd arrived.

"Hey, you okay?" She jogged to catch up.

"Yeah, I'm good. Just tired." How many times had I said that? It was losing its punch just like the words 'I can't' had failed me earlier.

Evelyn stopped next to me when we were well into the shadows. It felt safer here. Away from the light and curious glances. The sounds of the campfire and murmuring pack members faded slightly, replaced by the rustling of leaves and chirping frogs. "I didn't mean to interrupt Rowan's speech."

Evelyn shoved her hands in the pocket of her sweatshirt. "He won't care. He's just trying to bring people together. Make them less afraid."

"Are people afraid?"

Evelyn sighed. "How could they not be? After what happened?"

Fair. I hadn't thought much about it. I used to think about people besides myself, didn't I? I wanted to be that girl again, but these days, the pain was all-consuming. I couldn't come up for air.

Evelyn reached out a hand. "I'm sorry—"

I flinched, wincing and pulling my arm back.

Evelyn frowned. "What the hell was that?"

I dropped my arm to my side, trying to keep my expression even. "Nothing."

"You flinched like I slapped you."

"I have a bruise—"

"We don't keep bruises." Evelyn's eyes shot to mine. "Show me your arm."

My heart rate skyrocketed. "I'm wearing my jacket—"

"Show me your arm, Calli." Evelyn crossed her arms over her chest. The sound of boots on dry leaves sounded behind us, and we both turned to see Rowan's silhouette in the orange glow of the fire.

He looked between the two of us. "What's going on?"

Evelyn nodded to my left side. "Callista has something wrong with her arm."

Rowan's brow pinched. "From tonight? Let's take a look."

I wanted to run. *Why was she making such a big deal out of such a tiny motion?* I wanted to bolt past them and get in my truck and drive, but I knew that wouldn't accomplish anything. Rowan could outrun and outdrive me, and if I turned and ran back in the house, I wouldn't put it past Evelyn to break the door down. She'd gone after her crazy ex, and Nathan Black was a hell of a lot scarier than me.

"It's not a big deal—"

"Take off the damn coat!" Evelyn barked.

"Someone hasn't had their french toast," I muttered, pulling off my jacket and rolling up my sleeve.

"I wonder whose fault that is." Evelyn took a step closer as I revealed the bandages. I didn't wait for her to boss me around a second time, I just started pulling at the gauze.

SIX

"Callista—" Evelyn's words died in her throat as she held my arm toward the firelight and saw the wound.

"What the hell?" Rowan leaned in, his expression turning to stone.

Evelyn held the underside of my arm, rotating it to get a better look. "How did this happen?" I gave her a look, and her jaw slackened. "This has been here for three weeks?" Her head snapped to Rowan. "I thought Finn looked her over?"

Rowan's frown deepened. "He did."

I nodded. "He treated this like any other wound. He cleaned it and stitched it. But then...it didn't heal."

Rowan blew out a breath. "I'd like him to see it. There are too many strange things happening for this to be a coincidence. Is that okay with you?"

This was why I didn't want to say anything. This was why I didn't want Evelyn or even Blake to see my arm. They would make a big deal out of it when there wasn't a solution. "You two are making me feel like a stupid teenager."

"I hate to be the one to say it, but you did hole up in your house and *forget* to mention a festering wound on your body." Evelyn crossed her arms over her chest.

The idea that I could forget was laughable. The pain in my arm was constant. It turned my body into a three-year-old smartphone with zero battery life and a glitchy home screen.

"Take her to our tent. The lantern is on the ground by the entrance." Rowan turned and stalked back to the fire, and I obediently followed Evelyn past the bear bins to their postage stamp of land. Evelyn retrieved the lantern and set it on the picnic table, then turned it on high. I blinked at the bright light.

Finn and Rowan crunched across the gravel.

I managed a weak smile as Finn stopped next to me. "Let's take a look."

I lifted my arm, and Finn's eyes widened. He sucked in a breath. "Holy hell."

"Yeah." I exhaled.

"I treated this." He kept staring at it like if he watched long enough, it would start to make sense.

I looked down, my stomach turning at the sight. The edges of the wound were a deep, angry red. It was like a brand, searing my flesh.

Finn's fingers hovered over the wound, and I flinched as a wave of heat radiated from it. He muttered something under his breath, then looked up at Rowan, his expression grim. Rowan nodded without him even needing to say a word.

Finn dropped his hand. "I'll get you the supplies you need. I can definitely help with the pain and discomfort."

I nodded, starting to get antsy. Finn couldn't solve this. The only way I was going to figure out how to heal was by talking to someone who understood the dagger, and that was nobody currently standing around the picnic table.

Blake had gone with Evelyn and Rowan to the witch in the woods. He'd told me about their visit, and while she'd answered some of their questions, they hadn't asked the right ones. Not for my purposes. She was at the top of my list for having answers, especially since she'd provided Rowan with a tincture that knocked Nathan flat.

But whenever I thought about driving east into the woods, that weight landed back on my chest. The ache had tugged and pulled, drawing me north, and now I was right where it wanted me. There was no more strain, just...silence. I clenched and unclenched my hands. I loved the break from the pain, but I didn't like that whatever darkness the dagger had transferred was pleased.

Evelyn worried her lower lip. "I could take you back to Black Lake. We could call Brandon and get him to open the pharmacy—"

I looked between her and Rowan, noting his furrowed brow. "Pretty sure your mate has something to say about that."

Evelyn didn't have to look at Rowan to know I told the truth. He wouldn't let her get two meters from him, and he had a pack to combine. He couldn't shirk his responsibilities and run after me a second time.

I started re-wrapping the gauze. "I'll be fine. I'll—" I paused mid-sentence as Lana walked up next to us.

"Ready for bed?" She glanced around the circle, either completely unaware of the tension or ignoring it. I'd never been happier to see my roomie slash star of the TV show Alias. Even if I was still terrified of her.

"Yep. Absolutely. Exhausted." I finished wrapping and

pulled on my jacket. I had more supplies in my toiletry bag, I could make it look pretty in the...gross washrooms. Fantastic.

Lana handed me my toiletry kit as we walked down the road away from the lantern. "Found this in the truck. Assumed you'd want it."

"You assumed correctly." Was she being nice to me? "Thanks for saving me back there."

"They're like mother hens. I can see why you kept blowing them off."

Again, ouch. But not wrong.

The small bulbs flickered above the washroom doors, casting a dim, yellowish light that barely cut through the darkness.

I wrinkled my nose as we approached, the smell of pit toilet and air freshener hitting me like a wall. I pulled open the door, wincing at the creak of the hinges, and stepped inside. The air was stale, and the amenities bare bones, but at least there was running water. I used the toilet, holding my toiletries under my arm, then washed my hands and face at the sink. After brushing my teeth and drying my hands, I removed the old bandage and re-wrapped it, putting on a healthy squirt of antibiotic ointment. Because that was helping.

When I stepped back out, Lana was waiting, her flashlight beam dancing over the ground.

We stopped at the water pump on the way back and filled up her water bottle. The air was cool and crisp against my skin as we returned to the campsite. We stowed our toiletries in the truck and crawled into the tent, dropping our shoes on the dirt outside the entrance. I tucked both pairs under the tent flap and zipped us in.

I kept my clothes on as I climbed into my sleeping bag. It was the end of August, which meant the temps would drop below comfort levels overnight. When I was finally settled on the mat, that same strange calm spread beneath my skin.

"It doesn't feel the same. Being out at night." Lana's disembodied voice filled the tent.

I knew exactly what she meant. I used to love the dark sky. The stars. Now it felt almost claustrophobic. We'd been through nearly a full moon cycle since that night in the woods, and we weren't any closer to figuring out who Nathan was working with and what they wanted.

"Rowan talked with the alphas up north," Lana said.

I pushed up on my elbow, surprised that my arm barely complained. "When?"

"A few days ago. One of them finally returned his call."

"And?"

Lana shrugged. "It's bullshit. We know they were involved. Nathan was up there too often for them not to know what he was planning."

"You think he planned it all himself?"

Lana drew a deep breath. "You tell me. Do you think Nathan's smart or patient enough to find a relic?"

I snorted. Nathan was strong but more like a bull in a china shop. All rage and brawn, not so much brain.

I adjusted my sweatshirt around my waist. "What happened in the woods when Rowan killed Nathan?"

Lana's eyes flickered. "It was intense. Nathan was using dark magic, his power was palpable."

I nodded. "I felt it, too." I'd been out of it but still lucid during parts. The night came back to me in flashes. Disjointed. Like an abstract painting.

I took a deep breath, the air suddenly feeling thick and heavy. "When Nathan first approached me, I..." My voice trembled, and I closed my eyes, forcing myself to continue. "I was scared. Terrified, actually. I didn't know what he wanted, and when I found out—" My throat closed up, and I swallowed hard.

Lana didn't move, giving me space to gather my thoughts.

"He was persuasive," I continued. "Charming, even. At first, I thought maybe I was imagining things and just being paranoid."

"Yeah. That's how they get you." Her sleeping bag shifted. "I dated a narcissist once. Now, I can spot them from a mile away. Enjoy your new superpower."

I breathed a laugh. "Is it worth it?"

"Hell no. But it's a silver lining."

I smiled, dropping back onto my pillow. "I wanted it to be over."

Lana let out a breath. "That's why we're here, right?"

I nodded. An ending. That's what I was seeking. But as the ache in my wound continued to settle, I couldn't shake the feeling that being here was the opposite. I closed my eyes, trying to shut out the images that flashed behind my eyelids. I took another deep breath, forcing my muscles to relax.

I'd been led here for a reason. Whatever magic lived within me because of that damn dagger, it wanted me here. For better or worse, I was as close as possible to the force that might set me free.

But how would it do that? I shuddered. What was a dagger used for?

I shook my head, trying to clear the fog. I needed to rest. I wasn't alone, and whatever came in the morning, Lana and I would search for answers and hightail it back to Kitimat and Black Lake.

CHAPTER
SEVEN

KAEL

I jolted awake, my senses heightened, my heart pounding. The night was still, but I was immediately aware of the energy vibration. The power of the blade. The strangeness of its pull.

I willed my heart to slow, but my fingers twitched as I reached for it under my pillow. The force pulsed, reverberating through me, and I gritted my teeth, forcing my hand to still. Forcing my mind to clear. Probably not the best idea to have this thing next to my head while I slept.

The blade was dark as night, the hilt polished black metal. The clear stone embedded in the center seemed to glow in the black night.

I slipped out of the bedroll and pulled on the shirt I'd shed before bed, then slid one arm through the sleeve of my leather jacket. I hooked the clasp at my neck and pulled on my boots.

I wrapped my fingers around the hilt of the dagger, shivering at the contact, then pushed through the flap of the tent. The night air was cool against my skin, and the forest was a dark blur around me.

I half expected the dagger to pull me into the trees, but it didn't. I walked north, parallel to the road. My chest tightened, and I forced my feet to move, one in front of the other, as I followed the pull.

I didn't know what I was searching for or how long I was going to have to walk. Already annoyed with the lack of information, I wished I'd been smart enough to grab my bag so I could shift. Instead, I broke into a jog.

I didn't know how long I ran. Minutes? Hours? Time seemed to stretch as the night blurred around me, and I was lost in the pull.

I didn't care. If the dagger was coming alive, there was only one thing that made sense with my limited knowledge. Whoever's blood had been spilled on this blade, the blood it was seeking, had to be close.

That would save me another day of driving and a jaunt through Kootenay Pack territory, so I wasn't complaining. I could end this now and move on to the next pack.

I slowed as lights appeared through the trees. Washrooms. This was a campground. The pull drew me toward the path, but I stayed in the cover of the trees. I pushed through a thicket of bushes, the branches scratching at my arms and legs as I moved like a cat stalking its prey.

Ahead of me were dark campsites, and the dagger pointed to a small tent next to a firepit. I crept along the edge of the clearing, my eyes scanning the shadows for any movement. The energy thrummed in my veins.

I paused, my gaze landing on a truck parked a few steps from the tent. My body moved on instinct, my form low to the ground as I approached. The truck was old, the paint chipped, and the tires caked in mud. I peered through the window, my eyes adjusting to the dim light.

I saw slip-on shoes on the floor mat. Too small to be a man's. I scanned the dash, my breath catching when I saw the charm hanging from the rearview. It was a small wolf, intricately carved from wood.

A shifter? It wasn't definitive, but it was likely.

There was a jacket in the back seat. Feminine. Sunglasses. Gender neutral. Nothing in the truck screamed, "I have a big-ass boyfriend." Not that I couldn't take a big-ass boyfriend, but it made everything cleaner if I didn't have to.

I stepped back from the truck, my eyes scanning the area around the tent. No large tracks. The footprints were consistent with the size of shoes in the truck, though there were two different patterns in the dirt.

Two women, most likely. It was a three-man tent. They were cozy unless they were small.

I didn't love how that felt. Me creeping into a tent with two she-wolves.

I wasn't a mindless killer. I had rules. I only took contracts where I knew the world was better off without the people I hunted.

But this was different.

Destin had debts with the Alliance, and I owed my life to him. He'd literally changed my diapers as a pup, and he never called asking for help. I had to finish this, and when I did, he'd be free to walk away. We both would be.

There were no signs of movement, no sounds of life other than the rustling of the leaves in the breeze. They were asleep or MIA, but judging by the slight heat coming off the firepit, I'd bet big on them being inside the tent.

The dagger hummed in my palm, but I slipped it into my

jacket pocket as I crept closer to the entrance, my muscles coiled and senses on high alert. I took another silent step forward and crouched, my hand reaching for the flap. I paused, my fingers hovering over the fabric. The power thrummed in my veins, the dagger's call growing stronger.

I used my foot to hold the tent fabric and pinched the zipper between my finger and thumb as I pulled it up slowly. The motion was virtually silent, but even if they stirred, it wouldn't matter. I'd move fast enough that they wouldn't have time to fully wake.

The dagger's pull was an invisible thread, and I followed it, my senses heightened. My normal range of emotion seemed to drop beneath a steel floor, and a cool calm spread through me as my wolf prowled at the surface. I'd done this too many times to count. I was a predator. This was my prey.

The dagger tugged me to the left, my grip on the hilt tightening as I fought against the compulsion. I needed to be sure—to understand. My wolf pushed forward, and my vision sharpened.

There were two figures, one on each side. I hovered, my heart slow and steady in my chest. I took in the woman lying before me. Her features were gentle, and peaceful in sleep. Soft hair cascaded around her face, framing delicate cheekbones and full lips. I swallowed hard, my throat dry as I stared at her. Her body was relaxed, her chest rising and falling with each breath.

I hesitated, that floor cracking the tiniest bit. This wasn't my usual target. She looked innocent. Vulnerable.

I clenched my jaw, forcing myself to focus. I shifted forward and pulled the dagger from my pocket. Heat radiated from the blade, and it nearly yanked from my hand.

I leaned forward, adjusting my weight on my knees, and froze as a jarring sound filled the tent. Bells clanged together, their harsh tones shattering the silence. I held perfectly still until I caught movement.

What the hell was happening? *Move.* I needed to—

I spun, my eyes locking onto the bedroll in the corner. The other woman was already moving, her body springing up from her makeshift bed. Her dark hair whipped around her face as she lunged toward me, her eyes blazing with fury.

I threw myself backward, but the dagger refused to follow. My arm twisted painfully in my shoulder socket.

"Drop it!" the woman snarled, sending a kick to my midsection. I grunted as her hand shot out, her fingers wrapping around my wrist. She was strong but not strong enough. I rolled my shoulder into her, throwing her back as the dagger twisted in my grip, the blade slicing through the air.

And then I saw her.

The woman I needed to kill opened her eyes, jolting from her sleeping bag. My wolf scrambled back, howling in confusion, and the dam broke, my emotions surging through me like a tsunami. *She was mine.* I needed her. I—

The dagger tore forward as the other woman in the tent slammed into my side. I rolled, and we flew through the open tent door.

"Who the hell are you!" The dark-haired woman fought her way from the ground and kicked toward my wrist.

I let her.

The dagger flew from my grip, skittering across the gravel.

The blade wanted her blood, but I couldn't take it. My wolf thought the woman in the tent, the woman I was supposed to kill so I could fulfill my contract, was my mate.

CHAPTER
EIGHT

My vision wavered, the world around me blurring at the edges. I blinked, trying to focus, but the throbbing in my head made it impossible. My thoughts were sluggish, my senses dulled, as if I were moving through a dense fog.

The call of the dagger was physical, a gnawing ache that spread through my chest and into my limbs. I wanted to scream, to claw at my skin to make it stop, but I was trapped in my own body, a prisoner to its demands.

This was why I was here. The silver glint of the dagger replayed in my mind's eye, and I tried to take a step forward, but my legs wouldn't obey. I was frozen, my muscles locked in place as if held by invisible chains.

What was happening outside the tent? Helplessness washed over me, a wave of despair that threatened to drown me. I was powerless against the dagger's call, a puppet dancing on its strings. The pain was relentless, an all-consuming fire that burned through me, and if I didn't do something soon, it would consume me completely.

Then suddenly I was moving. Flying forward. I dove through the side of the tent, landing on the dirt in front of Lana and the intruder scuffling.

I only had eyes for one thing.

I locked onto the dagger in the dirt ahead of them and launched to my feet. It was there. I needed to—

A strong hand clamped around my ankle, dropping me to the ground. I spun, my eyes stinging from the scrape of gravel across my knees and the palms of my hands. "Let go of me!"

I clawed at the stranger's arms, my nails digging into his skin, but his grip was unyielding, even as Lana worked to wrest his arm back to his side.

I blinked. Did he only have one arm? Or did Lana—

"She's going to hurt herself!" The man growled. "The dagger seeks her blood!"

Lana hesitated. "What are you talking about?"

"She's marked, cursed."

Lana's eyes burned as she scanned my face. "Callista—"

"Let me go!" I kicked as hard as I could, and the man grunted. His hand flexed just enough that I pulled my leg free. I only got a few feet before he landed on top of me. "Lana!" I cried for her, fighting him with everything I had, but she didn't answer. He was too strong.

"Stop." He somehow gathered both my wrists into his one hand and pressed them to my lower back. "I don't want to hurt you—"

"Says the man who snuck into our tent!" I seethed, my cheek pressed against the dirt. I tasted sand, breathed it in.

Why was he doing this? Why wasn't Lana stopping him? "I need it. I need to—"

"Stop." His voice came from just behind my ear.

I kicked and twisted, but he held me tight until my strength began to wane. My arm felt like it had been boiled in acid. Sweat poured from me, soaking my clothes, and tears leaked over my cheeks.

Lana dropped to her knees next to me. "Callista, please explain—"

"I can't." My voice was a whisper, the words barely audible. "It hurts."

Kael's grip loosened slightly.

"What can I do?" Lana asked.

I shook my head, my mind spinning. I didn't know what to do. The pain was unbearable, a constant gnawing at my insides. I wanted to claw at it, to tear myself apart and end it.

Lana stood and walked to where the dagger lay in the dirt. I whimpered as she crouched and lifted it from the ground.

And it all stopped. The pain, the burn, all of it. Gone.

I closed my eyes as my entire body drooped.

"Callista." The man knew my name. I drifted, the relief so stark that it nearly put me to sleep. "Hey." He patted my cheek.

My eyes fluttered open. "What did you do?"

He stared down at me, his brow furrowed. "I didn't do anything."

"The pain. It's gone."

He looked up, then moved off of me, his hand still loosely circling my wrists. "Can you stand?"

I nodded, my throat tight, but when I tried to push up from the ground, my arms gave out.

"What's your name? And who sent you?" Lana started the inquisition.

"Kael." He ignored the second question as he looped his

arm around my waist and tugged. With his help, I steadied myself on all fours, then lifted to my knees. He stood and pulled me with him.

I didn't want to touch him. He'd been in our tent, he'd tried to kill me, and he'd brought that thing—

Rowan charged into our site, his dark hair tousled from sleep. Jasper and Will emerged right behind him, their eyes wild, raring for a fight.

My alpha crossed to us in three steps. "Drop her."

Kael stiffened. "I can't—"

"I said drop her!" Rowan sent a jab to Kael's jaw, and he stumbled back.

I, once again, landed hard on my knees in the dirt.

CHAPTER
NINE

Kael

The alpha gripped Callista to his side as we pushed past the trees, his chest heaving with barely contained rage. Asshat. He was the reason Callista was bleeding. My wolf growled.

Yeah, I want to kick him in the nuts, too. I mentally put a hand on his muzzle. There would be time for that later.

I followed him and his two lackeys into the underbrush.

Callista walked a few paces back, her eyes glued to my back. The weight of her gaze was like a physical touch, and it took everything in me not to turn my head and meet her eyes. I couldn't draw attention to her. To the way my wolf stirred at the sight of her. That feeling was nothing. A distraction I couldn't afford.

My jaw clenched, and I ran a hand through my hair. I didn't want to think about it. The idea of having a mate was ludicrous. I didn't belong to a pack, and I didn't want to. I traveled solo, and the fact that I was here in British Columbia proved that relationships were only a weakness in my line of work.

"Rowan, I think this is far enough," the Catwoman from the tent said.

The alpha slowed but didn't stop for another thirty seconds or so. When he found a small open circle between the trees, he handed Callista off to his brutish second and wheeled on me. "Explain."

"Explain what?" I shot back, my muscles tensing. I could barely hear my own breath above the adrenaline rushing through my veins. Anger. Anxiety. Fear. All of them swirled together into a toxic concoction.

The alpha growled, pointing at the dagger in Catwoman's hands. "Let's start with that."

I opened my mouth to respond, but she stepped in. "Let me give you the play-by-play, shall I?" She shot me an exasperated look. "I set a trap, he fell for it. Had the dagger in his hand, ready to stab Callista, and then I don't know what happened. He stopped, and Callista—"

My arms tightened at my sides, the muscle at the base of my jaw twitching. I wanted to shift. To let my wolf out and end this right here, but it was suicide. That didn't mean it wasn't tempting to go for Rowan's jugular. I didn't have a pack to leave behind. I didn't have anything to lose. But one look at Callista slumped next to him, and I held my ground.

Sweat trickled down my brow, and I wiped it away with my shoulder. The action instantly drew the others' attention. Their eyes snapped to the empty space beneath my T-shirt sleeve. I was used to people gawking. Curious or judgmental, I didn't care.

Still, I was ready to fight. Ready to tear into anyone who

came at me. I didn't know what this alphas plan was, but I wouldn't back down.

I couldn't.

Rowan's piercing blue eyes bored into me, and I wanted to melt into the ground. The alpha was a mountain of muscle, his frame taut with barely restrained fury. The man wanted to kill me. Wanted to tear me limb from limb, and I couldn't even blame him.

Catwoman stepped between us. Her eyes flicked to me, then back to her alpha. "Really, Rowan? Going full Hulk smash isn't going to solve anything."

"Back off, Lana." Rowan's jaw clenched, and his nostrils flared. The veins in his neck pulsed, and for a moment, I thought the alpha was going to shift and lunge at my own throat. But Lana didn't move, and Rowan finally stepped back, his muscles still coiled like a spring.

The younger wolf beside him stepped in, placing himself between Rowan and me. "We need him alive, Rowan. Killing him won't get us the answers we need."

Rowan's eyes narrowed, his lips pulling back in a snarl. "He threatened one of our pack. And he's got the relic."

Lana crossed her arms, her dark hair falling over her shoulders. "We need to know why. We can't afford to lose that information."

Rowan's chest heaved, his breath coming in ragged gasps, the internal battle playing out on his face. Instincts warring with reason. It was a struggle I was all too familiar with, and I half wanted the beast within him to win out.

Rowan fought for control. "Start talking, or I end you right here."

I didn't say a word. The silence stretched between us, thick and suffocating. What was there to say? My past was irrelevant. My intentions were irrelevant. I couldn't give him the information he sought, and I wasn't about to give Rowan or anyone else the satisfaction of hearing me plead or explain myself.

Rowan's frustration grew with each passing second. His nostrils flared, and his breathing became more labored. The muscles in his neck and shoulders tensed, his jaw working as if he were grinding his teeth to dust.

C'mon asshat. I clenched my hand into a fist.

"Who are you?" Rowan's voice was a hiss, barely a breath.

I remained silent. My gaze didn't waver. I could see the flicker of doubt in Rowan's eyes, the hint of uncertainty. It was enough to give me a sliver of satisfaction.

Then Rowan took a step forward, his nostrils flaring, his eyes blazing with fury. "I won't ask again."

I wanted him to hit me first. I couldn't make sense of what had just happened, and if I didn't let the frustration out, it was going to eat me alive. A fight was exactly what I needed.

"Rowan, stop!" A woman ran out of the trees, her eyes glinting in the moonlight.

Rowan turned so fast I knew exactly who she was. His mate. He put out an arm, warning her to stay back.

"That's him. He carries the scent I struggled to track." She pointed at me, panting.

Rowan stepped closer, his fists tight at his sides. His eyes narrowed, and I could practically feel the anger radiating off him like heat from a forge. "You killed them, didn't you?" His voice was a low, dangerous growl. "Those wolves in Kitimat. You were there with Nathan."

My mouth quirked, but I didn't bother responding. Rowan's body trembled with the force of his barely contained fury, his eyes boring into me, demanding I cower.

Just another alpha wanting to get into a pissing match. I'd seen it before, and I'd see it again. The silence that followed was heavy, pregnant with anticipation. The rest of the pack looked between Rowan and me, their expressions a mix of confusion and fear.

Rowan's jaw set in a hard line. "You need to explain yourself."

My heart hammered in my chest, and I inhaled for seven seconds to force it to slow. "There's nothing to explain. I followed the dagger."

"To kill us," the second added, his tone flat.

"I didn't touch your wolves." They wanted me to submit, to show my throat like a good omega, and it wasn't going to happen. I didn't kill anyone in his pack. Not yet, anyway.

"You just happened into the wrong tent then, eh, bud?" Rowan's second glared at me, his arms crossed over his chest so his muscles bulged. Very intimidating.

"Simple mistake." If my wolf wouldn't have surged, she'd be dead. I could've stopped her heart there in the tent, even with Catwoman's trap.

Rowan's jaw worked, but before he could spout out some other bullshit, Lana walked up to us.

"He had this." She held out the dagger, and Rowan took it from her. Instantly, Callista launched forward, feral and savage.

I spun, wrapping my arm around her and hoisting her off the ground. "Give it back!" I growled, and Rowan thankfully didn't have his head up his ass. He shoved the dagger back into Lana's palm.

Callista's body collapsed, just as it had before. She buried her head into my chest, whimpering, and my wolf surged to the surface.

"Get your hands off her." Rowan yanked my shoulder, and his second caught Callista before she dropped to the forest floor.

What was this? The burning inside my chest, the pull toward this woman I'd barely laid eyes on?

In the tent, I'd been sure it was a trick of the dagger. It wanted her, so I wanted her. Simple. Now, standing in the clearing, I wasn't so sure.

My wolf paced, growling low in his throat.

We were both confused. Addled by dark magic. The dagger had made me believe I had a mate, just like it had made me stay in this campground for the night. It was a powerful relic, capable of manipulating my thoughts, my desires. I would be glad to be rid of it.

"Please don't let go." Callista turned, still propped up by Bicep Boy. "When you hold it…" She exhaled, and her whole body moved with her breath. "It's the first relief I've felt since that night."

Lana blinked, turning the dagger over in her palm. "I don't understand."

"Did you ever touch it before?" Rowan's mate asked.

Lana shook her head. "But neither did any of you."

"I did." I shot Rowan a smirk, and his jaw flexed. "Just for research purposes."

A sharp pain exploded across my left temple, and I whirled to find Lana gripping the dagger backward, the hilt still facing me. "Looks like the dagger isn't partial. You know, for research purposes."

Blood dripped down the side of my face, but I didn't reach up to wipe it off. The cut would heal. I could wash my face when this shit show was over.

"Why did you go after it?" Rowan turned to Callista.

Callista looked at the dagger, and her reaction was immediate. Her body tensed, her breathing becoming more labored. "It's like… I don't know how to explain it. It feels like a magnet. Like I need to—"

She stopped short, and I knew the end of her sentence. I'd felt it. The blade called for blood. For death.

Lana frowned. "But you don't want to...harm yourself, right?"

Callista shook her head. "No. I don't want to touch it again, but every time you let go, my body is screaming at me to pick it up."

Rowan turned to his second. "Lyra said it wanted sacrifice."

Callista held out her arm and pulled up the sleeve of her shirt to reveal a gauze wrapping. "It gave me this wound." She kept her eyes trained on Rowan. "I think it wants to finish the job it started." She pulled away from the man holding her. "Thanks, Jasper. I can stand now."

Lana shrugged. "I don't know. But it's the only thing that makes sense. There's something about you that's connected to this dagger." She turned to me and held up the dagger. "Do you know how this works?"

My throat tightened. "No."

Jasper scoffed. "Convenient."

Lana shot him a look. "He might be a dickbag, but he kept Callista from grabbing it and stabbing herself." She turned back to me. "I want to know why."

I exhaled for seven. I didn't want to be here. I didn't want to be connected to these people, to Callista. I was there to finish the job and give the damn relic back to the alphas so Destin could go back to doing whatever the hell he did in Monticello.

Rowan crossed his arms. "I don't care about answers right now. We can get those from Lyra. I want to make sure he's not a threat."

The alpha posturing made my blood boil. It was always the same with alphas. They had to prove they were the biggest, the baddest.

Evelyn stepped closer, her eyes locked on me. "How do you mask your scent?"

I shrugged. "I've always been able to."

Evelyn's eyes narrowed. "Are you psi?"

"I'm nothing. Omega. I'm a thug for hire."

Rowan dragged a hand through his hair. "Jasper and Will, take the first watch. I want you and Lana on shifts. Two hours each. Don't let him out of your sight."

Jasper nodded, and Lana's mouth tightened into a thin line. They didn't like their babysitting assignments.

After an hour with me, they were going to like it even less.

CHAPTER
TEN

I pushed aside the tent flap, and my heart hammered against my ribs. My hands shook as I fumbled with the zipper. The tent felt both too small and too vast. He'd come in while I was sleeping. The dagger had led him right to me.

Every sound was magnified in the stillness. The rustle of leaves in the wind, the creak of the trees as they swayed. My eyes darted around, searching for threats that my logical mind told me weren't there.

But my logical mind had been wrong about a lot of things lately.

The wound on my arm was so still it was eerie. It had been calm before I slept, but when Lana held the dagger, I almost felt whole. That knot buried against my spine had loosened for the first time in weeks. It was almost more terrifying than the pain.

I squeezed my arms tighter around my knees, trying to ground myself. The dim light filtered through the tent fabric, casting ghostly shadows across my sleeping bag.

The tent flap rustled, and I gasped.

"It's just me." Evelyn's voice. "Okay if I come in?"

"Mmhmm." I swallowed, my heart in my throat.

She slipped inside and, after zipping the door closed, dropped to her knees beside me.

"Hey." She reached out to touch my shoulder. Her hand was warm, and I leaned into her touch. "You okay?"

"Trying to process what just happened."

Evelyn nodded, her auburn hair falling over her shoulder like a curtain. "You don't have to. Not right now." She shifted, sitting cross-legged next to me. "You don't have to make sense of anything."

I closed my eyes and rolled onto my back. "I thought I was going to die."

Evelyn twisted a loose strand of my hair in her fingers. "Remember when I was little, I was terrified of thunderstorms?" I nodded. "I thought the lightning was going to strike our house and burn it down. My parents used to tell me that the thunder was just the moon goddess and her mate having a wrestling match."

I forced a smile, for the first time able to plant myself back in reality. Evelyn's parents. She'd been worried about them accepting her after returning and staying in Black Lake. I didn't know whether she'd talked with them yet. "Did it work?"

"Yeah, it did." She grinned, her eyes crinkling at the corners. "I still think of that whenever there's a storm. Wrestlemania in the sky."

I blew out a breath. "So what you're saying is, I should imagine the man who snuck in here with a knife is actually—"

"Yeah, okay. Terrible comparison."

I laughed. "Kind of the worst."

"I just meant forces are working beyond us that we don't understand. That's comforting."

I grimaced. "Is it? Because I was happy living my mostly mundane life." I didn't rely on my wolf-like Evelyn always had. It wasn't that she wasn't there. I could feel her, and I never had any problems shifting, but comforting?

Evelyn lay back on Lana's pillow, and we stared up into the darkness in silence for a moment.

"You remember when we were kids?" I whispered. "How we used to sneak into each other's beds during those storms?"

Evelyn smiled. "Yeah. And how we'd pretend to be asleep when your mom or my dad came to check on us."

I nodded, the memory bringing a warmth to my chest that I hadn't felt in a long time. "Maybe it wasn't the worst comparison. This kind of feels like that."

I DIDN'T EVEN KNOW I was asleep until suddenly I wasn't. One second, I was curled up next to Evelyn, and the next, I was gasping for air. A rough hand clamped over my mouth, and I couldn't scream. Couldn't breathe. My eyes flew open, wild with panic, and I tried to struggle, but something held me in place.

Fabric replaced the palm across my lips, and the tent fabric parted beside me. I was yanked out of the tent, my sleeping bag still wrapped around me. I wanted to cry out, but my voice was trapped behind that gag. The world spun, and I flailed, trying to get my bearings.

There was no scent, and that's when I knew who it was. A second later, I made out his face in the moonlight.

Kael.

He loomed over me, his eyes cold and calculating. I barely had time to register what was happening before he pulled me from my bag and threw me over his shoulder. I struggled, but it was like fighting a steel beam. *How the hell was he this strong with only one arm?*

I'd been able to get a better look at him in the woods when I wasn't consumed with need for the dagger. He was missing his left arm from a few inches above where his elbow would've been. At least that was where his sleeve ended.

He was slightly taller than Rowan, and his hair was cropped short with the hint of a beard on his jaw. His eyes had looked gray in the moonlight.

Now I was only staring at the cotton blend of his long-sleeved T-shirt.

Kael didn't waste time. He took off, his strides long and purposeful. The motion jarred my senses, and I squeezed my eyes shut, praying this was some messed-up nightmare. It had to be.

Kael's grip tightened, and I cried out as his shoulder dug into my ribs. I looked back at the tent as he carried me away, and my heart clenched. Evelyn was still asleep in there, wasn't she? I had to get her attention before we moved too deep into the trees.

Where was Lana? Jasper? I tried kicking and pushing against his back, but it was like trying to move a boulder.

My lungs burned, and my breath came in short gasps, my body fighting for air as the cold night air stung my skin. The pounding of Kael's footsteps punctuated the hiss of air from my wheezing lungs.

I struggled, my thoughts a whirlwind. Why was he doing this? What did he want? My mind raced back to that night at Nathan's. How he looked at me. How he ran his thumb over the hilt of the dagger.

The dagger. My arm didn't ache. I didn't feel anything, which meant Lana still must have it. That or he'd figured out some other way to keep the dark magic quiet. What would he want with me if he didn't have the relic? I shuddered at that question.

Then, out of nowhere, a figure shot out from the trees, barreling into Kael with a force that sent him stumbling. I hit the ground with a thud, the wind knocked out of me. I gasped, my vision blurring. I forced my head up and caught sight of a familiar profile.

Lana. My heart surged.

Kael growled, his forearm snapping out to block Lana's next attack. She was a blur of motion, her fists and feet flying. I'd seen her in action before, but never like this. She was a force of nature, and for a moment, I thought Kael would be over-whelmed.

But then, with a snarl, Kael's body shifted. He moved with a fluid grace, his muscles rippling under his skin. His eyes glowed, his wolf pressing so close to the surface, I thought he might burst forth.

Lana didn't back down. She pressed forward, her move-ments a dance of calculated strikes and feints. I couldn't tear my eyes away from the fight, even as my mind screamed to run. To get as far away from this madness as possible.

Kael wasn't fighting. He was...but he wasn't. Not the way he should be if he were a hired killer. He was on the defensive, but he wasn't striking back. Lana stumbled, her back hitting a tree with a sickening thud.

Kael pulled me up from the ground as she stood there pant-ing, her breath visible in the cold night air. I wanted to scream, but the gag still made it impossible for me to do more than grunt.

"Leave us if you want her safe." He held me effortlessly. I

didn't have the strength to fight him after I saw how useless it had been.

Lana laughed. "You fought the dagger in the tent. I saw it. You're not going to hurt her."

Kael's jaw clenched, his breath hot against my cheek. "You don't know what I'm capable of." He shifted his weight, his body pressing against mine.

Lana didn't flinch. "You think I won't call your bluff?" She took another step, her voice steady. "Let her go."

Kael's grip tightened. "The dagger has a claim on her. I need to break it."

"Why?"

"It will help both of us. Callista will be free, and you won't see me again."

My wolf stood at attention when my name came out of his mouth. I'd forgotten he knew it.

"How do you plan to do that, considering we have no leads on this?" Lana pulled the dagger from her boot. She'd had it there pressed against her skin and didn't once reach for it.

So. They were both holding back.

Lana's voice was like steel. "I don't care what you think you have to do. You touch her, and I will end you."

Kael's eyes narrowed, and for a moment, I thought he was going to snap. But then he exhaled, his body relaxing slightly. "I know someone who understands the relics. But I take her alone."

Lana's eyes narrowed. "And why should I trust you? You came here with the dagger knowing as much as we do."

Kael's eyes darted to the darkness behind Lana. He flinched at a distant snap of a branch. "Because I have no choice. I allowed you to keep the dagger. That should be all the proof you need."

Lana didn't move, her expression unreadable.

Kael's grip tightened, and I winced. His breath was hot against my skin. "I don't have time to convince you."

I'd barely processed the words before being yanked deeper into the forest. The last thing I saw was Lana, her eyes wide as she cursed under her breath and followed after us.

ELEVEN

KAEL

Once I was sure we were far enough into the woods, I stopped, the pine needles crunching under my boots. I reached into my pack for a knife but decided against it. I didn't want to scare Callista, so I opted to untie the knot without tools.

My fingers slipped between Callista's skin and the fabric of the gag, and I unfastened it from the back of her neck. I pulled the fabric from between her lips. She gasped, her eyes snapping up to meet mine just as Lana stormed through the trees to stand next to us.

I didn't want her there, but I knew she'd go straight to Rowan if I forced her back. She'd probably already contacted him through their pack bond, but since he hadn't arrived with guns blazing, she must have sent some kind of a message to keep him away. That was good enough for now.

"Sorry, I—" I cleared my throat and rubbed the back of my neck. "We need to shift."

Lana worked to catch her breath. "Shift?"

"Yeah. I've got my truck parked a couple clicks that way." I motioned over my shoulder. "If we stay on two legs, it'll take forever."

Callista shook her head. "I can't." She looked at Lana, a plea in her eyes.

I frowned. "What do you mean you can't?" I sensed her wolf, so she had to be strong enough to do it.

It was Lana's turn to shake her head, this time with a touch of frustration. "Callista's wound. We don't know what will happen to it in wolf form."

I grunted. "It's not hurting now, is it?" In the woods with her alpha, she'd made it sound like when Lana held the dagger, the pain subsided. "It should disappear anyway."

Callista nodded. "Exactly. Our wolf form heals. Which is why I'm more worried about the shift back."

We needed to move. I wasn't interested in hypotheses about injuries during shifts. "Maybe shifting will help."

Callista's eyes flashed. "I'm not willing to risk my wolf being permanently injured. Plus, who knows where this wound will end up? I could have a partially severed artery in my wolf form. Do you know how dangerous that could be? I could bleed out before I even shifted back, and then what?"

I held up a hand. "Okay, okay. I get it." We were going to have to do this the hard way. I pulled out a length of rope and started to measure it. "Do you ride?"

Callista blinked. "Ride what?"

"Cats." I stared at her blankly until I realized she thought I was serious. "Horses, sheep, I don't give a shit. Something bigger than you?"

Callista shook her head. Great. We were going to do this

the really hard way. I pulled a switchblade from my pocket, cut through the rope, and threaded it through a carabiner. I set the knife between my teeth as I tied a knot with one hand, then looped the rope around my neck to pull it taut.

Both of them stared at me. I looked up as the rope slid from my shoulder. "What?"

"Nothing." Lana's eyes dropped, and I held back a grin. It was always the same. People were curious as hell as to how I managed with only one hand, but they weren't willing to ask questions.

I finished the knot, then repeated the process with a second length of rope, making a loop out of the carabiner for it to thread through.

"What is it?" Callista asked.

"Your chariot." I finished the knot, and that time, Lana and Callista didn't gape as I used my mouth.

"You're going to carry her? How?" Lana crossed her arms over her chest.

"Like this." I slipped the harness over my shoulders, setting the loops.

Lana raised a brow. "And you expect her to get onto your back?"

"That's the plan." I turned to Callista, who was staring at me, and a warmth sparked in my chest. It was a feeling I hadn't experienced in a long time. A feeling I didn't have time to dissect. "You okay with that?"

Callista's eyebrows shot up. "Do I have a choice?"

"Guess not." I started unbuttoning my shirt, then stashed it in my bag.

Callista's cheeks flushed crimson, and Lana snorted. "Can I use that, too?" She pointed to my bag.

I nodded. The idea of Callista watching me undress flooded my skin with heat, but I ignored it, reaching for my belt and yanking it open. As shifters, we didn't particularly care about modesty. Maybe these pack wolves were bigger prudes than I thought.

I kicked off my boots, then shucked my pants and underwear. I stashed everything in my bag and slung it over my shoulder.

Callista was turned away from me, and part of me was disappointed. One part in particular.

I let out a growl and shifted, my bones snapping and muscles shifting as my wolf form took over. I shook out my fur, then stepped into the harness.

Lana's eyes widened. "You can carry her on three legs?"

I barked and motioned with my head for Callista to climb on. My three legs were a hell of a lot stronger than Lana's four.

After a moment of hesitation, she moved. "Fine, I'm coming." She climbed onto my back and wrapped her arms around my neck, her legs gripping my sides. Pressure and warmth spread against my fur, and I shivered.

Keep it in your pants, I sent to my wolf. He was far too pleased with himself.

Lana shifted, her wolf form resembling more of a coyote than a true wolf. She was smaller, sleeker. She let out a huff, then turned and started trotting through the forest.

Callista's grip tightened as I snapped up my bag with my teeth and moved into a lope, my paws crunching against the pine needles. Lana's footsteps sounded behind me, her breath steady and even.

I focused on choosing a path through the trees, but I couldn't ignore the way Callista's heart pounded against my back, the scent of her filling my nostrils. I almost sideswiped a redwood. *Pay attention, idiot.*

"Wow, okay." Callista stiffened on my back.

What did she say? It sounded like a direct response to my

frustrated command to my wolf, which was impossible. I slowed to descend the river bank and tentatively pushed another thought. *Hold on.*

"Don't you want to add, "idiot" to that?" she sniped.

My mind spun. She could hear me. How could she hear me? Speaking in wolf form was reserved for pack mates and...

Blood rushed in my ears. *She is not my mate. She is NOT my mate.*

I bolted through the woods, trying to outrun what had just happened and trusting the harness to keep her steady. The rope bit against my belly as she jostled, but the sting kept me centered.

It wasn't until we reached the clearing where my truck was parked that I slowed. I waited for Callista to slide off my back, then shifted back into my human form and dug in my bag for my clothes.

I threw Lana's things to her and turned as she shifted and changed, then motioned for them to get in the truck. I slid into the driver's seat, and Lana took the passenger side as Callista slid into the back.

My wolf whined, but I ignored him and turned to face the two of them. "We'll be back by morning. Your alpha won't even know you're gone. Happy?"

Lana rolled her eyes. "Ecstatic."

I started the engine and pulled out of the clearing, the headlights cutting through the darkness. Callista shuffled in the back seat, and I caught a glimpse of her in the rearview mirror. Her eyes glinted, and she bit her lip. I swallowed, my throat suddenly dry.

I didn't want to think about how her hand had slipped from my neck when she slid off my back. I didn't want to think about how her breath had hitched when she felt my muscles tense under her. I didn't want to think about any of it, but the more I tried to push it away, the more it lifted to the surface.

I needed to break her bond with the dagger. Fast.

I clenched the steering wheel and sped. There was nobody on the roads at that time of night, and the drive to Fraser Lake was a blur.

We pulled up to the run-down house an hour later. "Here we are." I cut the engine and took it in. The paint was peeling off the siding, and the porch looked like it would collapse the second someone set foot on it.

Bill's son was probably using again. Not giving him any help.

Callista put a hand over the seat, and her thumb brushed my shoulder. "This is it?"

I nodded, then pushed open my door and dropped to the gravel drive.

CHAPTER

TWELVE

CALLISTA

Kael led the way up the wooden steps to the front porch. The boards creaked under our weight, the sound echoing in the stillness. A single cracked porch light gleamed next to the door, allowing me to see that the exterior of the house was rugged. It had weathered wood siding and a shingled roof that had seen better days.

It was just past midnight, and yet Kael didn't knock. He simply turned the knob and walked in. My heart skipped a beat at the audacity of it, but I followed him over the threshold. He removed his boots and stalked across the room, switching on the lamp on the end table.

The interior was cozy but cluttered. An old leather couch sat against one wall, flanked by mismatched armchairs. A threadbare rug covered the worn hardwood floors, and a coffee table was piled high with hunting magazines and empty beer

74

cans. The walls were adorned with hunting trophies, antlers, and black-and-white photographs of a man with a grizzled beard and kind eyes.

And there, in the corner of the room, was the face from the pictures. He was slumped in an easy chair, his head resting against the back, with his mouth slightly open as he snored softly. I should've been scared to be in a stranger's house, but Kael was so at ease I didn't think to panic.

The man's eyes snapped open as Kael's shadow fell over him. He snorted awake, his gaze darting around the room before landing on us. His face morphed from confusion to recognition and then to pure, unadulterated joy.

"Kael?" His voice cracked as he sat up, rubbing his eyes. "Is that you, boy?"

Kael nodded, a small smile tugging at his lips. "Hey, Bill."

Bill struggled to his feet, his limbs still clumsy with sleep. "Well, I'll be damned." He shuffled over and enveloped Kael in a bear hug, clapping him on the back. "I thought I'd never see you again."

Kael patted Bill's back, his expression softening. "You could've come up to visit."

Bill scoffed. "You wouldn't have been there anyway. I heard you were in the Ukraine? Egypt?" Kael's eyes flicked to mine as Bill finally pulled away. He looked at Kael like he was a ghost. "How long has it been? Five years? Six?"

Kael nodded. "Something like that."

Bill shook his head in disbelief. "Well, don't just stand there. Come in, sit down." He motioned to the couch, then his eyes narrowed as he took a proper look at me and Lana. "And who might these lovely lasses be?"

Kael's eyes darkened. "This is Callista and Lana."

My wolf stirred again, her ears perking up. She put me on high alert, hearing every creak of Bill's floorboards and the brush of Kael's shirt as he settled back into his chair. I breathed in the faint scent of pine oil and wood smoke.

My wolf wasn't going to make this easy, apparently. Every time Kael moved, she was right there, like I was dangling a raw steak.

I mentally ran a hand down the fur of her back. *It's only the dagger. We'll get that sorted, and you won't have to worry about this.*

She whined, but still, I felt more at peace than I had in weeks. It was like I'd been living my life in black and white and Lana, holding the dagger, had flipped the switch to high def. I could think again. Breathe again—

"You're grinning like a crazy person," Lana muttered as we sat on the couch.

I couldn't help it. I felt incredible. "It's just *such* a good morning."

Bill glanced toward the window. "Not morning yet."

Kael watched me a moment, assessing, then turned to Lana. "Show him."

Lana leaned forward, holding the dagger out in front of her. It caught the light from the lamp on the end table, and Bill froze. "Where did you get that?" His voice was a strained whisper, his eyes wide. He looked up at Kael, and his face drained of color.

Kael folded his arms over his chest. "It's a long story. Do you know anything about it?"

Bill shook his head. "Nope. Not a thing. Just that it's dangerous, and I want nothing to do with it." He tried to push up again from his chair, but Kael touched the man's arm.

"Considering how much you talked about Shadow Pack growing up, I'm calling bullshit."

Bill's gaze was determinedly fixed on the floor. "I told you. I don't know anything."

Kael's jaw ticked. "Remember when you caught me eating your expensive bacon in the middle of the night?"

Bill sighed. "That was a long time ago, Kael. I've moved on from—"

"And then I told you about my mother, and you let me sleep on your couch?"

Bill's eyes flicked to Kael's face. "I remember."

Kael's voice softened. "I trusted you with that, and you can trust me with this."

Bill's shoulders slumped, and he finally looked up. "Alright. But you have to promise me something, Kael. You have to promise me you won't use it."

Kael's eyes shuttered, but he nodded.

He was lying. He'd been about to use the dagger on me a few hours earlier, and he hadn't told us what the rest of his plans were. Did he have other shifters on his kill list?

Bill sighed. "Alright, then. I'll tell you what I know." He settled back down in his chair. "You know of the Shadow Pack?"

Lana nodded. "We've heard the stories. Some of them, at least."

Bill's eyes were fixed on the dagger in her hand. "Then you know about the relics. There were five of them in total, each with unique powers. The dagger you're holding is one of them. It was said to be the most dangerous of the lot."

Lana's eyes narrowed. "Dangerous, how?"

Bill leaned forward, resting his elbows on his knees. "The dagger's power comes from its ability to absorb the life force of those it kills. With each life it takes, it grows stronger, and its wielder gains abilities beyond those of a normal wolf shifter."

A shiver ran down my spine. I'd known the dagger was powerful, but absorbing life force? That sounded like something out of a horror story. It also made sense of what I'd seen with Nathan. His strength. His ability to control.

Bill continued, "The dagger was created by Seraphina, the founder of the Shadow Pack. She forged it from the bones of her enemies and imbued it with dark magic. It was meant to be a tool of protection, ensuring that the Shadow Pack would always have the strength to shield the world from dark magic."

I frowned. "But it holds dark magic."

Bill raised an eyebrow. "There's a story that's been passed down through the generations, one that might provide some insight. It's said that Seraphina had to make a great sacrifice to imbue the dagger with its power. A sacrifice that cost her dearly."

"What kind of sacrifice?" Kael asked.

Bill hesitated, then looked Kael straight in the eye. "Her mate."

The room fell into a heavy silence. Lana's grip on the dagger tightened, the wheels visibly turning in her mind.

Bill sighed. "It's just a story, mind you. And of course there was the legend of Thorne."

I pursed my lips. For all his protestations, he seemed to be enjoying the drama of his storytelling. "Who's Thorne?" I humored him.

His eyes sparkled. "Thorne was a powerful alpha who settled here in Canada when the land was still wild. Driven by the dagger's insatiable hunger for blood, he began a campaign of conquest, attempting to unite all the packs under his rule."

Kael shifted in his seat, and my wolf noticed.

Bill continued, "This alpha, believed to be a descendant of Seraphina, nearly succeeded in creating an empire, but his ambitions ultimately led to his downfall. The relics, once united in his grasp, turned against him. Shattering his mind and scattering themselves across the world. With the loss of the relics, the Shadow Pack fell into obscurity, and their secrets were buried with them. The few who survived went into hiding, and over the centuries, the legends of the Shadow Pack became the myths you heard at bedtime."

Lana and I exchanged a glance. *How was any of this helpful?*

Bill leaned back in his chair, his eyes heavy with the weight of the story he'd just told. "That dagger is a double-edged sword. It can grant you power, but it can also demand a price."

Kael nodded, his expression grave. "Thank you, Bill."

Bill waved a hand. "Just promise me you'll keep your head on straight, Kael. I don't want to hear any more stories about you running off into the night with a death wish."

Kael's lips twitched. "No promises."

Bill rolled his eyes, then stood up and motioned to the door. "Alright, then. You lot best be off. It's past my bedtime, and I need my beauty sleep."

I nodded, but as I stood, the room seemed to wobble. I grabbed onto the back of the couch, my vision swimming.

"Callista?" Lana's voice was muffled like she was speaking to me through a wall of water.

"Yeah. I'm fine. Just stood up too fast." I blinked, trying to clear the haze from my vision. When I glanced back at Kael, my whole body went tight. The room was too warm, and the air seemed to press in on me from all sides. My heartbeat pounded in my ears, and my skin felt like it was on fire.

I felt good. So good, I wanted to—

Oh, shit. *No, no, no.* The musk of Kael's skin hit me at full force, and my wolf responded instantly, pushing to the forefront of my mind. She was desperate. I was desperate.

This could not happen now. I couldn't—

"Callista, hey." Lana grabbed my shoulder.

I clenched my hands, trying to focus on anything other than the insistent pull I felt to cross the room and straddle Kael on the chair. My wolf was insatiable, and it was like she was trying to claw her way out of me to get to him.

I'd experienced plenty of heats before, but none of them had felt like this. It was as if my body was disconnected from my mind, and my flesh wanted to fuse with his. To touch him. Taste him. My wolf was howling, and I had to bite my lip to keep from doing the same.

"I have to get out of here," I groaned, spinning toward the door. My skin was too tight, my clothes too constricting. My wolf was pacing inside me, and I wanted to scream at her to settle the hell down.

I stumbled forward, knocking my shin on the coffee table. This was not how it was supposed to be. I was supposed to be in control, to be the one calling the shots. But with Kael in the room, I felt like a puppet with my strings being yanked.

Kael wasn't a match for me. *Not* a fated mate. He couldn't be. This was simple biology, and I just had to ride it out.

I bit the inside of my cheek. Poor use of metaphor. "I need a glass of water."

"Do you want me to get it for you?" Lana offered.

I probably looked like a drunk alpaca, but I shook my head. I had to get out of that room.

"The kitchen's that-a-way." Bill pointed to his right, and I stumbled into the hall. I walked toward the kitchen while my wolf surged inside me and caught the doorframe, forcing air into my lungs.

My thighs burned as I forced myself forward and grabbed a glass from the cupboard, then filled it with water from the tap. I drank, then splashed some of the water on my face. The cold was a shock, but it didn't do anything to cool the feverish sensation under my skin.

I set the glass down on the counter, then gripped the edge, my knuckles turning white. My wolf was pacing, her fur standing on end, and I had to fight the urge to rip off my damn clothes.

I needed to touch him. I needed to feel his skin against mine, to bury my face in his neck and breathe him in. The urge was almost unbearable, and I had to bite down on my lip to keep from crying out.

This wasn't me. It couldn't be. This was the dagger, or the moon, or something else. Anything else.

Lana appeared in the kitchen, her eyes narrowing at the sight of me gripping the counter for dear life. "What's going on?" she hissed.

"What the hell do you think is going on?"

She took in my labored breathing, the flush on my skin, the sweat on my brow.

Lana's eyes widened. "When was the last time you felt safe? Like, truly safe?"

I blinked. "What are you—"

Lana strode past me and craned her neck to peer out the window. "Damn it." She spun to face me. "It's almost full."

"Mmhmm." I squeezed my legs together.

"You've been under an insane amount of stress, and with me holding this, your body feels more relaxed."

"Right," I gasped.

"And then there's Kael—"

"This has nothing to do with him." I gritted my teeth.

She nodded once, her expression darkening. She knew what this meant as well as I did. Wolves were vulnerable in heat. Our hormones were all over the place. Back in Kitimat, I would've gone directly to the sweat house. I would've dropped into a hot tub with the other women and rested.

But I was currently in a shanty in the middle of shit nowhere, trying to keep myself from jumping the man who'd tried to kill me. "Lana, what do I do?"

THIRTEEN

KAEL

Her scent hit me like a battering ram. I gripped the coffee table, holding on for dear life as Callista's perfume filled my lungs.

My pulse pounded in my ears. This wasn't right. It was supposed to be Callista who got her panties in a twist when she was in my presence, not the other way around.

I flexed my fingers, wood splintering under my palms.

"Easy on the table, eh?" Bill's voice was a distant hum, barely registering through the chaos in my head. I forced myself to nod, even though every nerve screamed at me to turn back and find her.

She was right there. Just down the hall. *In heat.*

I clenched my teeth, resisting the urge to tear into the

kitchen and pin her to the floor. *What the hell was wrong with me?*

My nostrils flared as I inhaled deeply, my heightened senses picking up every nuance of Callista's scent. It was like walking into a bakery and being assaulted by the aroma of fresh bread, except this was a hundred times more potent.

I'd never been one to lose my cool, not since I was a kid, but Callista's scent was a siren call I couldn't ignore. It was intoxicating, a heady mix of warmth and spice that made my blood boil. I could almost taste it on my tongue, and the thought of it drove me to the brink of madness.

I could hear every whisper of her breath, every rustle of fabric as she moved. My mind conjured images of her, her skin flushed, her eyes half-lidded with need. My muscles tensed, and my wolf clawed at the surface, demanding to take control.

I'd never felt this way about anyone, not even during my teenage years when hormones raged like wildfire. This was different. Intense. Supernatural.

It had to be the dagger. Break that bond, and I was free of whatever the hell this was.

Lana stormed back into the room, her eyes blazing. "We need to find a place where she can rest."

I gripped the arms of the chair, my knuckles white. "A place where she can rest?" I repeated the words, my voice strained.

"Yes, Kael. Rest. As in, hiding her away so a wolf like you can't ravage her in the middle of the living room." Lana's voice was like ice water on a flame.

I exhaled. "I wasn't—" But I was. Every muscle in my body was coiled, ready to spring. I couldn't lie to her.

"There's a guest room down the hall. I don't think it's been used since the nineties, but it should be fine." Bill shoved his hands in his pockets. "There's a washroom across the hall. Probably best to get her some water, too."

Lana brushed past me, and I heard her voice down the hall. "Come on, love. Let's get you settled."

When Callista was behind a closed door, the heat inside me lessened, but not by much. I ran a hand through my hair.

Bill chuckled. "Seen that look before, pup." He leaned against the doorframe, his eyes twinkling with amusement. "Back in the day, when the she-wolves went into heat, it was like a damn circus. You couldn't walk two feet without tripping over a pair of wolves going at it like rabbits."

I shot him a look. "Thanks for that visual."

He grinned. "Just trying to lighten the mood, eh?"

I barely registered his words. The scent of Callista still lingered in the air, and I clenched my fist to keep from following it. From tearing down the hallway and finding her.

Bill's expression softened. "You know, there's one surefire way to ease the pain of the dagger. Until you can find a way to break that bond."

I exhaled through my nose, my hand landing on my hips. "What are you talking about?"

Bill met my eyes. "Mating, Kael. If you mated her, you could share the curse. Hell, it might even heal her."

I barked out a laugh. "That's not happening. I won't take a mate just because the dagger is messing with my instincts."

Bill raised an eyebrow. "You sure it's only the dagger?"

I shot him a glare. "What the hell else would it be?"

Bill shrugged. "I don't know, but you're not the one wielding it now, are you?"

I shook my head, my jaw working. "No, Lana has it."

Bill nodded. "And she said she'd neutralized the magic. So, if that's the case, why are you about to rip through your jeans?"

I rolled my eyes. "I don't know, Bill. Maybe it's because it's still close by? Or maybe it's because I've had it for the past week?"

Bill held up a hand. "I'm not saying I know the answer, but I do know this. Mating isn't something to take lightly. It's a bond, a connection that's deeper than anything else you'll experience. And if you think this is just the dagger making you crazy, you're missing the bigger picture."

"Which is what, exactly?"

Bill leaned back in his chair, his eyes narrowing. "You've always worked alone, Kael. Maybe your wolf is trying to teach you something."

FOURTEEN

CALLISTA

I stood under the icy stream of water, my hands shaking as I tried to keep my balance. The spray from the showerhead hit my chest, and literal steam rose from my feverish skin.

I was a mess.

My fingers fumbled with the shower knob, trying to turn it colder. The water was already as frigid as possible, yet it did nothing to quell the fire burning inside me.

This was it. This was how I was going to die. Scalded to death from the inside out. Ironic, really, considering the gaping wound on my arm and my aversion to heat. I'd always been more of a cold-weather girl, preferring snowy chill to oppressive summer heat. Appropriate, then, that I was craving an ice bath.

I closed my eyes and tried to remember the last time I'd felt anything like this. My first heat had been bad, sure, but not like this. It had been more of an inconvenience than an emergency, a biological reminder that I was, in fact, an omega. But this?

I leaned my head back, letting the water pour over my face. The icy droplets felt like needles on my burning skin, but I welcomed the sensation. I reached out and braced myself against the shower wall, my skin slick with water. The tiles were cold under my palm, a small relief from the heat, but it was like trying to put out a forest fire with a squirt gun.

I need a mate. The thought slammed into me like a freight train, and I squeezed my eyes shut, trying to block it out. My wolf whined, pushing against my consciousness. *No.* I could handle this. I'd dealt with pain worse than this over the past few weeks. I could wait it out.

My muscles tensed, and I fought the urge to curl into a ball on the shower floor. I didn't just need a mate. My wolf wanted him. She could sense him, even with the doors between us. Kael was seconds away, and she was desperate.

"He's not good for us," I hissed. He wasn't. He was a hired killer, working for the same people Nathan had been. I knew nothing about him besides that, and those details weren't favorable.

But would it be terrible to have someone take the edge off? I knew wolves who did that all the time. Who called one of our single men or even a human. My wolf growled, and an image of Kael flashed in my head.

"Not helping." *Damn.* She needed to settle down.

I turned off the water, wrung out my hair, and grabbed the towel hanging on the bar. I barely had time to register the rush of cold air before Lana stepped in, her dark hair pulled back, her eyes sharp with concern.

She closed the door behind her, locking us in the small, tiled space. "You've looked...better."

I tried to smile, but my lips barely moved.

Lana exhaled. "How bad?"

I forced myself to take a deep breath, but it felt like my lungs were filled with hot coals. "Worse than before. So much worse."

Lana shook her head. "I'm so sorry. I wish there was something I could do. Do you want something to eat? Bill says he makes a mean Kraft Dinner." Lana smirked.

I shook my head. "No. I just need a minute."

Lana nodded and leaned against the counter, her arms crossed over her chest. "Do you want me to stay?"

"No. You can go enjoy Bill's noodles."

"Well, when you say it like that..."

I laughed, still clutching the towel around me. "This is terrible timing."

"It's predictable timing," she said. I shot her a look. "Your body has been through hell, and now, with all this going on." She twirled her finger in the air. "You need to be careful."

My eyes narrowed. "The moon, right? The magic? That's what you mean by all this?" It's not like I could avoid the moon cycle or the fact that the dagger was hunting me.

"Definitely. It has nothing to do with the ultra-masculine wolf sitting in the other room."

"Lana!" I hissed. "This is not because of Kael."

"It's not *not* because of Kael. He saved your life back there."

"Yeah! After he tried to take it!"

Lana shrugged. "When wolves feel threatened, their instincts kick in. It's like a survival mechanism. Your body is trying to find a way to protect itself, to ensure you have someone strong enough to keep you safe."

"But Kael's not—"

"It doesn't matter what he is. Your body is reacting to him

because he's the one who found you, who brought you back to life. It's not about logic. It's about biology."

I frowned. "So my body is just . . . doing this without my permission?" I opened the washroom door, darted across the hall to my bedroom and flopped down on the bed.

Lana stormed in after me, slamming the door behind us. "*Careful.* I know this isn't what you wanted to hear, but it makes sense, doesn't it?"

I was already sweating again. "If he's still here, will this go on forever?"

"I hope not," Lana muttered. "As it is, Rowan's going to be pissed we left."

Rowan was the last thing on my mind. "Are you going to call him?"

She nodded. "Pray for me."

I groaned and sat, looking at my bag Lana had brought in from the truck and the pile of dirty clothes. "I should sleep."

"Can you sleep?"

"That is yet to be determined." *No.* The answer to that question was no. The idea of putting clothes on made me cringe, but the thought of getting into Bill's sheets naked... well. I hoped they were clean.

Lana retreated to the door. "Okay, but you know where I am. Just call, and I'll be here." I nodded as she exited, leaving me alone with my thoughts and swollen lady parts.

As soon as she left, I threw off my towel. The digital clock on the nightstand read one-thirty eight. Fantastic.

I flicked off the lights, then stripped the quilt and top sheet back on the bed. I curled up on my side, trying to convince myself that I could handle this. That I didn't need anyone else. That I didn't need him.

But my mind kept drifting back to Kael. I made up stories

about him. Pretended he'd looked at me in ways that he hadn't. That he'd touched me in places that weren't logistical.

Flashes of his eyes, his mouth, his *hand* played through my mind like a reel on an old film projector. He only had five fingers, and the things he'd been able to do with them were mind-boggling. They must be more dextrous...

And then there was the thought that sent my stomach plummeting.

Kael knew. He'd seen me run to the kitchen, and even if Lana didn't explain, male wolves were instantly aware of the change in scent when a she-wolf was at her height of fertility.

Was he in his room feeling this, too? Did he have the same insatiable heat running through his veins?

I hated that I wondered. That I was so desperate for release I was fantasizing about him.

Call him.

I froze at the thought. It wasn't words exactly, rather an impulse. A knowledge, pushed to me from my wolf.

I can't call him, I don't have his—

A rush of what I can only describe as colors and warmth burst from my mind, sent like a beacon meant for one person and one person only.

My wolf had just put out the equivalent of a red-light bat signal for Kael.

CHAPTER
FIFTEEN

I lay on the couch, staring at the wooden beams above me, my hand fisted around the quilt. It was soft and worn, made by Bill's late wife. She'd been talented with a needle and thread. I'd watched her as a pup.

The room was too quiet, too still, and my senses still too sharp. The faint whisper of the wind through the trees outside and the creak of the old house settling put me on edge.

None of it was a distraction from the real problem. Her scent. It laced the air, seeping into my lungs with every breath. I turned onto my stomach and buried my face in the pillow, but it was no use. I couldn't escape it. It was everywhere, wrapping around me like a cocoon.

Sweat beaded on my forehead, and my muscles tensed. My heart pounded in my chest, and I fought the urge to throw the quilt off and march down the hallway.

I'd just met her. I knew nothing about her except that she was supposed to be dead. I rolled to my side and had just forced my eyes closed when my mind exploded with light.

Kael.

My wolf bolted to his feet.

What. The. Hell.

It wasn't me, he seemed to say, and I squeezed my eyes tighter.

Another blast. It was coming from her. But how? I thought back to the run through the woods. How she'd heard me in her head.

She needs us. That was definitely my wolf. He was like a damn devil on my shoulder.

"She doesn't need us. She needs a mate, and that is not me." I gritted my teeth. This was insane. I gripped the quilt tighter, but with every wave crashing on the rocks of my mind, my resolve slipped a little more.

We didn't have to mate, did we? I'd heard from enough she-wolves how painful their heat could be. How all-consuming. If she just needed a little relief...

I rolled onto my back, adjusting myself in my pants. Maybe it didn't matter that we were essentially strangers. Maybe that made it better, actually.

My wolf was clawing at my insides, begging me to go to her.

It won't be what you want, I shot at him. He didn't seem to give a shit, and I took a shuddering breath. I couldn't hold out much longer.

The images of her standing in front of me morphed into fantasies. Her standing in front of me, her breath hitching as I stepped into her personal space. Her lips parting, her chest rising and falling. I pictured myself reaching out and touching her, feeling the softness of her skin, the warmth of her breath on my neck.

I imagined pulling her close, feeling her body press against mine. My hand sliding down her back, her breath hitching as I traced my fingers along her spine. I could almost feel her trembling under my touch, her heart pounding in time with mine.

Callista. Are you serious about this? I sent the thought, not sure if she'd hear me. I waited, my pulse throbbing in my throat.

Don't make me beg.

The need in her voice was like a drug, and despite my best efforts, I was already addicted. I was going to get strung out if I didn't get a fix. I stood, searching for my boots. I found them at the front door and slipped them on.

Lana's going to rip me a new one if I come within ten feet of you.

Lana was parked in the hall, right outside Callista's door. Going in that way wasn't an option.

Window.

My wolf howled at the sense of her voice. I stepped toward the door, and the floorboards creaked under my weight. I winced.

I took two more careful steps until I reached the door and pressed my hand against the wood. Every muscle in my body was taut as I turned the knob and cracked the door open, peering onto the porch.

My wolf growled in approval, and I stepped out into the night, closing the door behind me. I stood still for a moment, listening. No movement inside the house. No one had heard me.

I moved quickly along the side of the house, barely making a sound on the grass. My heart pounded in my chest as I approached the window of Callista's room. There was a faint light coming from inside, and my pulse quickened. A shadow moved. She was in there, waiting for me.

I reached for the window, but then I stopped, remembering the tent. Lana was in the hall, but that didn't mean she hadn't scouted out the guest room. I couldn't risk triggering one of her traps and waking the whole house. I took a step back and pushed a thought forward.

I can't open the window. You'll have to do it.

I waited. The light shifted behind the curtains, and the fabric was swept to the side. She was there. In nothing but her bra and underwear. She was curvy with hips that begged for my hand to curl over them.

Before all the blood rushed from my head to my groin, there was a click, and the window slid open.

I stepped forward, but before I could reach the sill, a door slammed. I froze, my heart in my throat.

"What the hell are you doing?" Lana's voice was a low growl. We were screwed.

CHAPTER

SIXTEEN

CALLISTA

"I needed some fresh air." I leaned casually against the window frame. "Wait, how did you know I opened the window?"

Lana narrowed her eyes. "It's not smart to have that open."

"Because if someone wanted to break in, they couldn't just smash through the glass." I gestured at the forest behind the house. "What's going to happen? There are no highways, no major cities, just a few small towns and plenty of trees and wildlife." And an extremely hot man who I hoped was out of eyesight.

Lana raised an eyebrow. "You don't think anything could happen in the middle of nowhere? Like, I don't know, something happening right in our campsite?"

My wolf growled, and I gritted my teeth. "I'm not a child,

Lana. You said you aren't a good babysitter, correct? I'll shut it when I can breathe."

Lana stared at me. "Wow. Your hormones grew you some balls."

I swallowed hard. My agitation was only growing with the scent of Kael wafting through the window. My wolf whined with need. I clenched my fists. "I'll be fine. I promise. And I'll see you in the morning."

Lana huffed. "Fine. But if anything happens, I'm telling Blake it was your idea." She marched to the door and walked out of the room.

I let out a breath and sagged against the wall. As soon as the door shut, I spun toward the window, searching for him.

He appeared out of the shadows, his eyes glinting in the light from my window. I stepped back and watched as his hand wrapped over the sill. He pulled himself up and swung his leg into the room. In seconds, he was standing there on the carpet, his presence filling the space.

My heart thrummed at the sight of him. My hands shook. How was I supposed to do this? I'd messed around with other betas before, but never with someone I didn't know. My wolf, so vocal seconds ago, slunk back, shy all of a sudden. *Thanks for nothing.* "You—"

"Don't want to talk." Kael's voice was a low rumble.

I swallowed hard, my skin tingling with anticipation. "Good, because I wasn't planning on it."

I drew a deep breath, the cool night air still floating in through the open window, mingling with the intoxicating scent of Kael. It was heady, like a blend of cedar and pine with a hint of smoke, and it made my head spin.

I stepped closer, the rough wooden floorboards pressing against the soles of my bare feet. If he could be bold, so could I. "Take off your shirt."

Kael's eyes darkened, his pupils dilating. He hesitated for a fraction of a second before reaching for the hem of his shirt and pulling it over his head. His muscles rippled under his skin, and I couldn't help but stare. My mouth went dry.

With that one action, we had an agreement. I was the one giving orders, and he was the one obeying. My thoughts raced. *Was I really doing this?* I was an omega from Kitimat, and here I was acting like some sort of dominatrix.

It felt good, to be honest. Even though I didn't have the first clue as to what I should do next with him.

Kael's breath quickened, his pulse jumping in his neck. He liked this. I could sense it. My skin tingled, my wolf practically foaming at the mouth. I wanted to close the distance between us, to run my hands over his chest and feel the warmth of his skin, so I did.

As my palms pressed against his skin, his eyes shuttered closed. "You don't—"

"Shut up," I snapped. He'd said no talking and my ability to process more than the heat flooding through my fingertips was nonexistent.

Kael's hand jumped to my hip, his fingers threading around the waistband of my underwear. He lowered his head, his breath hot on my neck.

"We're not mating," I whispered.

"I know." His voice was calm, but I could sense the storm shifting beneath his skin. "We're just dealing with this."

"Right." I swallowed hard. This was just about my need. The itch that was desperate for scratching. Nothing more.

Kael's grip on my waist tightened, and I bit my lip. I trailed my hands down his sides and pulled at his lower back, dragging him toward the bed. When my calves made contact, I sat, but Kael stayed put.

He lowered his eyes, taking in the curves of my hips and

thighs. The soft swell of my stomach. The way my bra pushed up my breasts. His breath quickened, his gaze roaming over my body with an intensity that sent heat pooling low in my belly.

I'd never been thin like Evelyn, and I'd always been self-conscious of my curves. But Kael seemed...appreciative.

Kael's fingers traced the line of my jaw, sending a shiver down my spine. I held my breath as he stepped back and unbuttoned his jeans. I'd watched him. When he'd taken them off before. But this was different. This was for me.

He dropped his jeans, then dragged his boxer briefs off his hips, disentangling them and stepping free.

Holy shit. I couldn't stop staring. When I finally forced my eyes to his, he had a lazy smile on his face. He nodded once at my bra, and I reached back and unclasped it, letting the straps slide over my shoulders until it puddled in my lap.

"Almost there." He stepped forward and tugged on my underwear. I lifted myself from the sheet, and he slipped his hand under my butt, pulling them off in one smooth motion.

I gaped at him. "How did you do that?"

He dangled the fabric on one finger. "I've learned to be creative."

I slid back on the bed as he climbed onto the mattress and settled next to me. I reached out and shut off the lamp.

Yes. That was better. As much as I wanted to drink him in, I didn't want to think. I needed to close my eyes and *feel*.

We lay there for a moment, our bodies pressed together, and I felt like I was going to explode from the inside out. Every nerve ending was on fire, every instinct screaming at me to do more. To take more.

I swirled my fingers over his tight stomach, dragging my nails through the hair that tempted me lower.

Kael's hand found mine, and he intertwined our fingers, his grip firm but gentle. His touch sent a jolt of electricity through me, and I gasped. Kael moved, his body pressing even closer to mine.

"Callista . . ." He whispered, hot against my neck, and my eyes rolled back in my head.

I couldn't take it anymore. I needed more. My free hand reached up, sliding over his shoulder and down his back, feeling the ripple of his muscles beneath my palm. Kael groaned, and satisfaction surged through me. I was affecting him just as much as he was affecting me.

I rolled my hips against him, and Kael's breath hitched. His grip on my hand tightened. "Tell me how I can help." His lips brushed against my ear.

"You're already helping."

He grinned against my cheek. "I think this might be making it worse."

He wasn't wrong. *How could he help?* I wanted everything. I wanted to be consumed. I wanted to drown in him. But everything wasn't an option. Not unless I wanted to regret this even more than I was surely already going to. "Touch me."

Kael didn't hesitate. His hand slid down my side, leaving a trail of fire in its wake. When he reached my hip, he paused, taking his time with those last few inches.

I sucked in a breath when he landed.

"Like this?"

I nodded, my breath coming in short gasps. "Mmhmm."

Kael's breath hitched. My skin tingled with anticipation, and I arched my back, pressing against him.

Yes. My curiosity about that damn hand was rewarded. He was gentle and rough, teasing me and then giving me exactly what I wanted.

"Kael—"

"Shh. Lana's still outside the door."

This was going to be impossible. How could I keep myself

from crying out? I buried my head against his shoulder, pressing my lips against his skin.

For weeks, I'd been a shell of myself. I'd gone through the motions. Work, food, sleep. A neverending cycle that drained the life from me. In one day the pain in my arm had lifted, and now *this*.

It was a blur of sensation. Kael's hand on my skin, his breath hot against the top of my head. I couldn't think, couldn't breathe, couldn't do anything but feel.

Kael pulled away, nudging me onto my back. He didn't ask permission as he slid down the bed, his hand trailing over my thighs, his breath hot on my skin. "Tell me if you want me to stop."

"I don't. Want you to stop." I shivered as he reached my knee, nudging it out with his shoulder, and I squirmed, my hands clutching at the sheets. "I—" My words were cut off as he pressed his lips to my skin, his tongue tracing a line up my thigh. The sensation was electric, and I arched my back, a moan escaping my lips.

"Quiet, Callista." Kael's hand gripped my hip, holding me in place as he continued his exploration. I was lost in a sea of sensation, rising higher than I thought possible, then dipping and crashing against the rocks.

He was relentless. Consistent. The tension that had been building inside me, that coil winding tighter and tighter, suddenly reached a breaking point. It was too much and exactly enough.

"I know we said no talking," he murmured, his voice thick with desire. "But now I need to hear you. Tell me—" His fingers traced circles, teasing me, driving me mad.

"I want you here. Next to me." The words came out as a whisper, but he understood perfectly. He slid back into place next to me and pulled me to his chest.

When his hand found me again, he was done with teasing. As my back arched, he leaned in, pressing his lips to my ear. "I've got you. You can let go."

With those words, the dam broke. I felt a rush of heat, a wave of pleasure that crashed over me, drowning out everything else. My body convulsed, and I turned my head into the pillow to keep from crying out.

Kael didn't stop, didn't slow. He rode out the storm with me, his touch never wavering. When the waves finally subsided, I collapsed against him, my body trembling.

"Better?"

I fought to keep in the wave of emotion crashing over me. As a tear slipped over my cheek, I was glad the light was off. How had I felt so safe? So protected? Hours ago, Kael had a dagger to my throat, and now?

Kael pulled his hand away, and I whimpered at the loss.

"Kael, I—"

"Shh."

"It was good."

"Callista—"

"I need you to know how good that was."

He chuckled. "I *am* capable of reading body language."

"Thank you."

He was quiet for a moment. "You're welcome."

We lay there, our breathing deepening, and I worked to gather my courage. When he pulled his hand away from my shoulders, I caught his arm. "My turn."

SEVENTEEN

KAEL

I stiffened as Callista's fingers trailed down my chest. The sensation of her touch was electric, sending jolts of pleasure through my body.

This wasn't how it was supposed to go. I was here for her, but every time I tried to tell her she didn't need to return the favor, she wouldn't hear it.

I struggled to tamp down the urge to bolt for the window. I was always the one in control. As tantalizing as it had been to let Callista lead, we both knew where it was heading. Now my wolf bristled at the idea of being vulnerable, of being touched. But each brush of her fingers was intoxicating, making my blood run hot.

My heart pounded in my chest as Callista's hands moved lower, her breath warm against my skin. I could barely think straight, my thoughts a jumbled mess of desire and hesitation.

I was teetering on the edge, and one wrong move would send me plummeting into a free fall of lust.

Callista was saying something. Her voice was a soft murmur, and I forced myself to focus on her words. "You're shaking."

I hadn't even realized it. My hand trembled at my side, and I sucked in a breath, trying to steady it. "I'm sorry—"

"Why the hell are you apologizing?" She looked up at me through her lashes, the moonlight now pouring through the open window. "I like it." Her hands moved up to my shoulders, and she pushed me back against the pillows. The warmth of her body against mine was a welcome distraction, but it did little to quell the tension coiling in my gut.

Callista's fingers traced the lines of my muscles, her touch featherlight. "You were so good at that." Her voice was so low I had to strain to hear it. Her eyes sparkled with mischief, and I couldn't help but smirk.

"You mentioned that."

She nodded, her hands slipping lower. "I've never been able to just relax like that. I felt . . . safe."

Safe. The word hung in the air between us. She had to be joking. I was the last person in the world who should've been able to make her feel safe.

I suddenly felt like a fraud, like an asshole taking advantage of her. That's what I was, wasn't I? I knew better than to crawl into bed with a she-wolf in heat, and yet I'd come running the second she'd called.

"Callista—"

She pressed her hands against my thighs. "Stop trying to make me change my mind."

My mouth clamped shut. She moved over me, and I closed my eyes, feeling the weight of her body against mine. Her skin was warm, her breath hot against my neck, and I struggled to keep my wolf in check.

But it wasn't just him. This was what I wanted. What I needed. And it terrified me.

Callista's fingers trailed along my abdomen, and I sucked in a breath, my muscles twitching under her touch. She moved lower, and my heart slammed against my ribs. I couldn't think, couldn't focus on anything other than the sensation of her skin against mine.

Her hand slipped lower, and I groaned, my hips bucking involuntarily. Callista stilled, and I opened my eyes to see her staring at me, her hazel eyes wide and filled with concern. Her lips parted, but no words came out.

I reached for her then, my hand wrapping around her wrist. "It's okay," I murmured, my voice hoarse. "I'm just . . . not used to this."

Something flickering in her eyes. "You work alone."

That one sentence. The way she looked at me. I swallowed hard and nodded. "You don't have to do anything you don't want to, Kael. I just thought—"

"I want to." My grip tightened on her wrist, and I pulled her hand back to my abdomen.

She nodded again, her eyes searching mine. Worry was etched in her features, and it made my chest ache. I didn't want her to feel like she was doing something wrong.

Callista leaned down, pressing a kiss to my abdomen, and I sucked in a breath. Her lips were soft and warm, and the sensation sent a shiver down my spine. She moved higher, planting kisses along my chest, my neck.

Warmth bubbled up in my chest as my tension bled away, replaced by a heady mix of desire and gratitude. When had I been touched like this? Kissed like this?

Callista was giving me something I didn't know I needed.

She was inviting me to let go, to be vulnerable. Just like I'd told her to be.

My heart thundered in my ears as Callista's hands explored, her touch both soothing and teasing. My body screamed for more, but I forced myself to stay still, to let her lead.

She shifted, her body pressing against mine, and I couldn't hold back. I reached for her, my hand tangling in her hair as I pulled her lips to mine.

I hadn't planned on kissing her. That had felt more intimate than what we both had agreed this was. But I couldn't stop myself.

Callista moaned into my mouth, and the sound sent a jolt of electricity straight to my core. I deepened the kiss, my tongue exploring the warmth of her mouth as my hand roamed over her back.

She arched into me, and my wolf growled in approval. It didn't feel right to only take. Even though I'd already been given free rein, it wasn't enough. I wanted her to feel as good as she was making me feel.

Callista pulled back, her breath ragged, and I watched as she moved lower, her lips trailing down my chest. I was trembling, my muscles taut as a bowstring as she kissed her way back down my abdomen.

She hesitated, her eyes flicking up to meet mine, and I nodded, giving her permission to continue. Callista's breath hitched, and I could see the want in her eyes. She wanted to make me feel good. She wanted to give me the same pleasure I'd given her. And I wanted to let her.

She leaned down, her hair falling like a curtain around her face as she pressed her lips to my skin. The sensation was electric, and I clenched my teeth to keep a groan from escaping.

We're not mating.

How had I been so sure I didn't want to? How, from standing outside the window to now, had my mind started to change?

My thoughts flashed back to Bill in the living room. Maybe your wolf is trying to teach you something. This? This was what I'd been missing?

It wasn't only physical, not for me. With each press of her lips, Callista was breaking me wide open. Exposing a soft center I didn't remember existed and couldn't pretend to contain.

She was shattering me.

Molding me.

I was putty in her hands.

I dropped over the edge, fisting my hand in her hair as my body shuddered. She held me. Her hands gripping me as I sank into the bed, my breath coming in ragged gasps. Callista kissed me. Once. Twice. Then climbed up next to me and threw her leg over my hips.

For a moment, neither of us spoke. The room was filled with the sound of our breathing, the scent of sweat and arousal still hanging in the air. It was intoxicating.

Next to me, Callista wore a gentle smile, her eyes half-lidded. Her hair was a mess, and her lips were flushed. She looked like she'd just woken up from a nap, and the thought made me smile.

She shifted, and I felt a flicker of guilt as she pulled the sheet up to cover herself.

I reached out to brush a strand of hair from her face. "That was incredible."

"I *am* capable of reading body language." She shot me a cheeky grin.

Shit. The way my heart jumped in my chest. Not good.

Her expression fell a little.

"You okay?" I asked.

She nodded, but her eyes were still a bit wild. "Mmhmm. I've just . . . I've never . . ." She trailed off, her brow furrowing.

I waited, giving her space to find her words. It was a rare thing for me.

"I've never done anything like that before," she finally admitted, her cheeks flushing deeper. "Not with someone I just met. Not with someone I don't even really know."

"I'm sorry, I—"

"No, don't apologize." Callista shook her head. "I wanted it, and it was amazing. But I don't know how to process it."

I nodded, understanding more than she probably realized. "I get it."

She looked at me, her eyes searching mine. "Do you? Because I feel like you look totally calm while I'm lying here naked with a guy I've known for less than twenty-four hours, and I'm trying not to freak out because I don't want to ruin this moment, but also my brain is screaming at me to run."

A laugh bubbled up in my chest. "Yeah, I get it."

Callista's eyes softened. "How do you do that?"

I frowned. "Do what?"

"Make me feel . . ." She hesitated, then shook her head. "Never mind." Callista's lips pinched, and then her shoulders started to shake. I didn't know what to do. I wanted to comfort her, but I was afraid of making her feel more awkward. Then her hand shot up to her face, and I saw her blinking rapidly. The tears welling in her eyes made my chest tighten.

When they started to spill over her cheeks, I couldn't stop the sound that rumbled in my chest. It was something between a growl and a whimper, and before I knew it, I was pulling her against me.

The warmth of her skin flooded my senses as I guided her down to my chest. Her head rested on my shoulder, and the steady rhythm of my heartbeat thrummed against her cheek. I wanted to wrap my arms around her, to cocoon her in my embrace, but I held back, afraid of crossing some invisible line.

My fingers found their way to her hair, and I stroked it gently. "Hey, it's okay," I murmured, my voice barely a whisper. "You're okay."

Her shoulders shook harder, and I felt a pang of something deep and primal. It was more than just empathy. It was a visceral need to make her pain stop. The pull toward her was stronger than ever, but I didn't know what else to do.

It was like her pain was a knife slicing through my chest. I wanted to roar in frustration, to demand that the universe fix whatever was making her feel this way, but I knew that would only make things worse.

"It feels so good," she murmured against my skin.

I frowned. It was the last thing I expected to hear out of a woman's mouth when she was actively crying. "What does?"

"Life. This. You. All of it. I didn't think I'd ever get to feel this again." She sighed. "I think...I don't want to die, Kael."

My chest tightened. "You're not going to die."

"Ironic."

Yeah. It was. But it was true. I had no idea what the hell was going on or how to fix it. But I knew one thing for sure: I couldn't stand the thought of her being in pain.

She tilted her chin, and her eyes searched mine. I hoped she could see the resolve there. "You can't control this."

I saw the silent question there. *Did I want to control it?* "I can try."

Callista's lips twitched. "I'm going to take a shower." She pushed up from my chest, then stopped. She considered her words, then said, "Stay."

So I did.

All night. Or what was left of it anyway.

I hadn't meant to stay until morning, and when I woke with her in my arms, I was horrified at how right it felt.

I couldn't have a mate. I couldn't get used to this.

She moved as if sensing I was no longer sleeping, her cheek nuzzling against my chest.

"Good morning." I smoothed her hair from her eyes.

"Good—" Callista tensed. Her eyes flew open.

I paused, pulling back at the sound of an engine coming up the road. Tires crunched on the gravel, and I knew exactly who it was.

Rowan had noticed his pack had dwindled during the night.

CHAPTER

EIGHTEEN

K ael dressed fast enough to qualify for a world record. It was barely past nine in the morning, but I felt like it was six. How much sleep had we actually gotten?

Kael paused to give me a last look that set my blood on fire, then headed for the window. I leaped out of bed, smoothed the sheets, and tossed the pillows back into place. Because somehow I thought that a mussed bed would prove I'd been tangled up all night with Kael rather than simply sleeping.

The sheets weren't the problem. Kael's scent was *everywhere*. All over the bed. All over me. Kael was already halfway out the window, his muscles flexing as he braced himself against the frame.

"Bye!" I yelped, then clapped a hand over my mouth. *Bye?* What the hell kind of send-off was that after the night we had?

I was such an idiot.

Kael gave a terse nod, then disappeared from view. I took a deep breath, then continued my frantic tidying. Clothes scat-

110

tered, sheets in a tangle, and my adrenaline spiking higher than a CPU clocking into overdrive right before a system crash.

I froze mid-swipe when a sharp knock sounded at the door. My heart pounded in my chest. I couldn't open that door. Not smelling like him.

"Hey, I was just getting in the show—"

Lana pushed the door open, and I skittered back behind the bed. Her eyes immediately narrowed as she took in the scene.

I forced a smile. "Good morning."

She didn't answer immediately, her eyes scanning the room one more time. "Rowan and Jasper are here."

My heart skipped a beat. Rowan *and* Jasper? I immediately panicked. "I'll be right out, but I'm a mess. I need to put myself together and...take care of things. Down there." I waved my hands over my crotch.

Lana frowned, but she moved out of the way as I grabbed my clothes and toiletry bag, then rushed past her into the washroom.

I threw a quick, horrified glance in the mirror. My face was flushed, my hair a mess. I looked like...I'd just had sex. A lot of it. *Excellent.*

I stripped off my clothes, tossing them into a heap on the floor, then turned on the shower. The water cascaded down, and I jumped in, scrubbing furiously. I needed to get rid of Kael's scent, to erase any evidence of what had happened between us.

Even though I didn't want to. Not yet, anyway. All morning, I'd waited for the embarrassment and self-loathing to hit, but it was disturbingly absent.

After washing my hair and rinsing, I stepped out of the tub. Realizing I'd left my towel in the other room, I used the hand towel to dry myself, then wrapped it around my hair as best I could and got dressed. These clothes didn't smell like him, and I was beyond grateful I'd chosen to throw in an extra set.

I pulled on the shirt and pants, then ran a hand through my damp hair, hoping to look at least a little bit composed. Lana must've informed Rowan about my situation. If he said a damn word, I'd have a free pass to send a snarky reply his way.

I walked out into the living room, my senses on high alert. Bill was already in the kitchen, cracking eggs into a pan. Rowan and Jasper were standing near the front door.

It only took a second for them to pick up on my scent, and the shift in their demeanor was immediate. Rowan's piercing eyes locked onto me, and I could see the storm brewing behind them. Jasper's usually relaxed posture went stiff, his gaze darting between the room and me.

"Where is he?" Rowan's voice was low, his anger barely contained.

I swallowed hard, my mind racing. "I don't know what you're talking about."

Jasper's eyes narrowed. "Kael. Where is he?"

I forced myself to meet their gazes, even though every instinct told me to back down, to look away. "I haven't seen him."

Lies. I never lied to my alpha. The words twisted in my gut.

Rowan took a step closer, and the air seemed to thicken. "Callista—"

"I said I haven't seen him. Am I the one on trial?" I planted my hands on my hips.

Rowan's nostrils flared. "No. I'm sorry. For everything. We need to get you out of here. Away from—"

"With all due respect, that's not happening," Lana stepped forward. "Not for at least another day."

Rowan's eyes flicked between the two of us. "Why not? It's

not safe for you here. We can protect you better at the pack house—"

"I know, but . . . " I avoided his gaze, my mind a whirlwind of thoughts. I didn't want to go. Why didn't I want to go? I didn't relish staying here at Bill's, but the idea of returning to our pack made me cringe. "Not yet. We need to figure out how to break the bond."

Rowan frowned. "We can do that at home. We can go to Lyra—"

"When I was a pup, I heard legends about the Shadow Pack relics. Stories that most dismissed as fairy tales." Bill stalked out of the kitchen.

Rowan exhaled sharply. "Who is this?"

Bill put out a hand, and Rowan shook it. "The name's Bill." He adjusted the waistline of his pants. "That dagger is growing stronger. You can't just pluck her out of here and hope for the best. It will fight back. If it's growing in power, it won't let her go without a fight."

Rowan looked to Lana. "You said you had it under control."

She nodded once. "I do. For now." Her eyes dropped. "There's no precedence for this. We don't know why it's responding to me, and we don't know what to expect."

Bill nodded. "The stories say that it will work on any soul it comes in contact with. I—" He stopped, glancing up as Kael sauntered down the hall. He stopped when he saw all of us gathered ahead of him.

His hair was damp, and he wore a clean T-shirt and jeans. My heart skipped a beat at the sight of him. Rowan ground his teeth.

Bill seemed oblivious to the tension between them. "Kael, you're taking the wind out of my story."

"Which one?" He leaned against the wall, and my ovaries twitched.

Bill cleared his throat. "I was working up to it. Giving a little mystery before I gave the full meat of it."

Kael grinned, then glanced up at me before steeling his expression.

"Can we get on with this? Please?" Jasper snapped, and Kael looked like he'd be glad to put a fist to his throat.

"Jasper." Lana shook her head.

Bill motioned for them to take a seat. They reluctantly took off their shoes and moved into the living room.

When they were settled, Bill dropped into his chair and started with a deep breath, his chest expanding under his flannel shirt. "Alright, here's the gist. The Shadow Pack was a group of shifters from way back when, tasked with guarding the veil between the living and the Shadow Realm. They were descended from a forbidden union, giving them unique spiritual and shadow abilities. They were entrusted with powerful relics, but internal conflicts led to their downfall. Despite their end, their legacy and the relics they guarded became the stuff of legend."

Rowan nodded. "I've heard the stories."

There was a twinkle in Bill's eye. "Good, good. Then you know that if the relics reappear, it means something. Something big."

Lana frowned. "Big, how? Big as in restoring the Shadow Pack?"

"Or destroying it for good, depending on who gets their hands on 'em," Bill replied, his voice low and grave.

"The Shadow Pack doesn't exist now," I said.

Bill raised an eyebrow. "They surely do." He turned to look at Lana. "They're hidden among us. Descended from that ancient line. Sometimes we know who they are before they do."

I pretended to be distracted by breakfast as Lana paced back and forth across the worn wooden floor of Bill's living room.

Her jaw was tight. "This is ridiculous. Shadow Pack? Those are just stories we heard as pups."

Bill blew out a breath. "Well, if you have a better explanation for why that dagger's behaving like a docile pup when you touch it, I'm all ears."

Lana's jaw clenched. "I don't know, maybe it's broken." She traced the edge of the blade. "Or maybe it's reacting to my natural charm."

Jasper grunted. "Sure, Lana. Your charm. That's definitely it."

Bill's eyes met hers, then he leaned forward, planting his elbows on the armrests. "Believe what you want. But the relics don't lie. That dagger didn't still for you because it was feeling generous." He pointed at her. "You're related to the pack where Seraphina's mate ruled. Her power recognizes you."

"That's all fine and well, but what do we have to do to destroy it?" Rowan asked.

"Well, that's the tricky part, isn't it?" Bill sighed. "The relics were created for a purpose, and until that purpose is fulfilled, they can't be destroyed. At least, that's what the legends say."

Lana scoffed. "So we're stuck with this cursed dagger until the end of time? Fantastic."

I scooped eggs onto my plate, then almost dropped the spoon when I heard Callista's voice.

"No, I think Bill's exactly right."

Bill chuckled. "Of course I'm right."

"Do you have a computer?" Callista asked.

I waited with bated breath for that answer. The last time I talked with Bill about technology, he was convinced radio waves gave us cancer.

"In here." Bill led Callista down the hall, and the others followed. I carried my plate to the hall. Bill's house was small, and I wasn't going to be caught dead in close proximity to Rowan or his second. I could hear just fine from where I was.

I closed my eyes as Callista's scent hit me. It was still strong. She was probably still uncomfortable. Probably still needed...easing.

I shook my head, trying to clear the image of her eyes fluttering shut, her body arching under my touch.

"What are you looking at?" Rowan asked. I took a few steps further down the hall.

Callista answered, "I found this online. Before we went camping. I didn't have time to read all of it, but..." She paused a moment, then said, "Yes! Here. Look at this."

It was silent too long. I was about to turn the corner when I finally heard her voice again.

"It says here that the relics were always meant to protect the Shadow Pack. So what if..."

I couldn't help myself. I shoved the last spoonful of eggs into my mouth and stalked forward. "What if, what?" Rowan, Jasper, and Lana turned to me with scowls. "Don't be pissy. If you want me gone, I need to hear this just as much as you do."

Callista pushed back from Bill's computer, turning in the chair. "What if it would respond to not just my blood, but one of its own?" Lana's expression flickered, and Callista stood, her brow pinching. "I don't mean a full sacrifice. I would never ask you to give your life for mine. But I wonder if it would be satisfied with less if it was the blood it was made for in the first place."

Bill pointed at the computer screen. "The legend says the curse of the relics was acquired through greed. We all know what that means." He straightened, scanning the room with a triumphant expression.

We blinked at him.

"I, for one, do not know what that means," Lana muttered, leaning back against the wall, the dagger still in her hand.

Bill groaned. "Think. It's the basic premise of our magic. Our power evolved in reaction to dark powers surging in the world. It's Newton's third law. Every force—"

"Has an equal and opposite reaction," Callista finished, chewing on her lower lip. "It's a deadlock."

Lana frowned. "What the hell is a deadlock?"

Callista folded her arms across her chest. "In a deadlock, two or more processes are stuck, each waiting for the other to release a resource. It creates a standstill. The more you try to force them to proceed, the more they lock in. But if you do the opposite—by breaking the cycle and releasing resources or rolling back one of the processes—you can resolve it. They'll run smoothly."

Rowan nodded. "So don't give it the blood it seeks."

"Give it a selfless act. The blood it was made to serve." Callista fixed her eyes on Lana. "You don't have to—"

"I want to." She pursed her lips. "I want to try."

Jasper dragged his hand through his hair. "And if this doesn't work? Then what, the dagger will kill both of them?"

My wolf growled. *We're not going to let anything happen to her*, I promised. I still didn't know how to reconcile the last twenty-four hours. I couldn't take a mate. It wasn't my nature. But holding her in my arms had sparked a desire for that life.

I turned and stalked back to the kitchen and rinsed my plate. *What the hell was I thinking?* The alphas still held Destin, and I had a contract to complete. Of course it sounded fun to play house. To ignore my real life and drown in pleasure for a night.

Why the hell wouldn't that be fun?

And now I had a bigger problem on my hand. They wanted to try neutralizing the dagger with Lana's blood. If it worked, Callista would be free.

But I would never get that dagger again. Hell, it might not even work the way it was supposed to. I had to use the dagger to save Destin's life. I had to give up the dagger to save Callista's.

Destin was like a father to me.

Lana paced into the kitchen. "So, I just what? Drag the blade across my wrist?" Bill and Callista stood in the doorway, the two thugs behind them.

Bill blew out a breath. "Whatever you do, it should be at a place where the veil is thin. Give it the best chance of satisfying the magic."

Callista shuddered. "Please don't say—"

"Swan Lake." Bill frowned at the expression on her face.

My nostrils flared. She didn't like that answer. Why? My wolf stood at attention, just as curious as I was.

"I need to call Evelyn. Let her know I won't be coming back as planned." Rowan pushed to his feet.

Lana frowned and glanced at Jasper. "Rowan, we can't all be here."

I liked Catwoman better and better. The faster these two left Bill's the happier I'd be.

"I don't think we have a choice."

"I'm the one with the connection to these relics, and I'm more than capable of taking care of this." Lana crossed her arms.

Rowan glared at Kael. "If I go, he goes, too."

"The dagger is mine," I growled.

"It's a relic. It doesn't belong to anyone," Rowan snapped.

I straightened. I was at least half an inch taller than him, and I wanted him to know it. "It's in my charge. The only reason your third has it in her possession is because I'm not a sadist." Callista's cheeks flushed pink, and my skin tingled. "Where the dagger goes, I go."

Rowan ground his teeth. "Then I'm staying."

"Fine by me." I leaned back against the counter.

Callista put her hands on her hips. "Can we all take a breath, please? It's a gorgeous morning. For the first time in weeks, I have hope that I won't be condemned to a lifetime of pain, and we've been with Kael for the last fifteen hours." Her eyes flicked to mine, and I could've sworn her breath caught. "He's done nothing to harm—"

"He took you from your damn tent! He tried to kill you!" Rowan's eyes glowed, and I suddenly wanted to meet him chest to chest. I gripped the edge of the counter.

Callista swallowed. "It was in the opposite order."

Jasper scoffed. "Does that matter?"

"Yes!" Callista shouted. "Something happened, okay? And as you can see, I'm fine—better than—"

"What happened?" Rowan gripped the back of the chair in front of him.

Callista stilled. She glanced at Lana who looked up at me with a questioning look.

Shit. How was I supposed to explain why I was ready to slit her throat one second and protecting her the next?

I coughed. "I needed to make sure it was necessary."

Rowan turned to me. "What, her death?"

I nodded, turning back to the sink. I picked up my plate and squirted it with dish soap.

Rowan took a step closer. "You want me to believe that when you're hired to kill someone, you *double-check* before murdering them?"

I stopped mid-scrub and met his eyes. "If you don't double-check a murder target, what would you double-check?"

Callista stepped between us. "This is a messed up situation. Fighting with each other isn't going to help."

Rowan's jaw clenched. "I don't like the idea of you being alone with him."

"That's not your decision to make." Callista's eyes narrowed. "I'm not your pup, Rowan."

"Doesn't matter."

I rinsed my plate and set it on the drying rack. "I want to help. If there's a way to clear her blood from the dagger, I'll help."

"And then?" Rowan's voice was low.

I dried my hand on the towel on the counter. "Then I go on my way."

"With or without the dagger?"

My throat went dry. I forced myself not to look at Callista and opened my mouth, but before I could answer, Rowan's phone rang. He pulled it out of his pocket, and his expression shifted the second he looked at the phone screen. He stalked out of the kitchen.

"Hey, baby." He paced in the living room, then stopped, his eyes widening.

"What is it?" Jasper stepped past Bill, and Lana was right behind him.

Rowan didn't answer. He kept listening to the voice on the other end of the line, his knuckles turning white as he gripped the phone. Finally, he twisted it away from his mouth. "It's Marissa. She's having her pup, but they're still on the drive home from the campground. We're the closest ones to her."

Jasper's eyes widened. Lana tucked the dagger back into her waistband and covered it with her shirt. But my mind was far from the kitchen.

I was staring at the moon, and my breath clouded in the frigid air.

Twelve years ago.

The night I'd been abandoned by my pack.

I was six years old. It was a clear night, the moon high in the sky, and I stood at the edge of the clearing alone. The cold had seeped into my bones, and even as a young pup, I knew I couldn't stay there. I had to find shelter, food, something to keep me alive.

I trudged through the snow, my boots crunching with each step. I'd been crying, and the snot in my nostrils was turning to ice.

"You look like you've seen better days." A grizzled man with the lightest eyes I'd ever seen stepped out of the trees. I didn't have the energy to startle.

He motioned for me to follow him, so I did. We came to a

small cabin nestled in the trees. I followed him in, and my life changed forever.

Destin was retired special ops from across the border. He lived off the grid, and he took me in. Fed me. He never once asked about my past, though the fact that I only had one arm probably made it obvious. Over the next few months, he taught me how to survive. How to hunt, fish, and find shelter. How to navigate the forest and mountains. He showed me the plants that were safe to eat and the ones that could kill me.

When I was older, I traveled with him to visit rogues. One night a she-wolf went into labor. I was terrified, but Destin insisted I jump in and help instead of hiding in the corner of the room.

The cabin was small, the air thick with the scent of wood smoke. She lay on a makeshift bed, her mate pacing the floor. Destin guided me through the process, showing me what to look for, when to encourage her to push. It felt like a split second and an eternity, but eventually, a tiny head emerged. Destin worked quickly, and soon, a squalling pup was in his arms.

I'll never forget the father. How he dropped to his knees, tears streaming down his face. Destin handed him the pup, and he cradled his newborn, his shoulders shaking.

That had been the first time.

Life is precious, Kael. Out here, we have to fight for it every day. Never forget that.

I blinked. "I can do it."

Rowan's head snapped up. "What?"

I met his gaze head-on. "I know how to deliver a pup. I've done it before. Three times, with my own hands. I've assisted plenty more."

"Don't you mean hand? Singular?" Jasper quipped. Lana elbowed him in the ribs, and he muttered an apology. I didn't want it. Wolves had been underestimating me my whole life because I didn't look like them. I couldn't wait to prove this asshole wrong, too.

Desperation flickered in Rowan's eyes. "And I'm supposed to trust you with the life of a packmate?"

I didn't flinch. "Do you have a better option?"

He glanced at Jasper and Lana, then blew out a breath. "Fine. But if anything happens to her—"

"It won't." I reached for my boots and called to Bill, "We'll need whatever medical supplies you've got. Anything in the trucks that could be useful—towels, blankets, clean water."

Bill nodded, already moving. "Got a first aid kit in the back of mine."

"I've got one in my pack," Callista offered.

Jasper and Rowan hurried out the door and went to their truck. Lana took a load to mine as Bill grabbed the last few things from the washroom inside.

Callista started to follow, but Lana shot her a look. "You're not coming."

"Bull shit." Callista didn't hesitate. She stomped across the driveway.

"Callista—"

"I feel fine, Lana. This is more important, and I'm not staying here alone."

I dropped a stack of towels in the bed of my truck. "Her alpha's right there. Who's going to mess with her?" I risked a glance at Callista and was rewarded by that damn flush of her cheeks.

"Do you have everything?" Jasper called out. Bill shoved a bottle of iodine and a bucket of clean rags in the back seat.

I nodded. "Let's roll."

CHAPTER

TWENTY

Callista

I didn't wait for Kael to stop the truck before I leaped out the door and sprinted into the trees. Lush ferns brushed against my legs, and branches snagged my clothes as I pushed through the underbrush. I didn't care. I needed to get to Marissa.

I knew what it felt like for my body to be out of control, and I couldn't imagine having to stop on the side of the highway to give birth. She had to be terrified.

My ears strained for any sound of the others. Rowan and Jasper had gotten ahead of us by a few minutes.

"This way," Lana called.

I shifted direction, my boots struggling for traction on the moss-covered logs. If I slipped, I was going to bite it hard. My arms were filled with supplies, and there was no way I'd be able to catch myself.

Somehow, I stayed upright, and a few seconds later, we saw them. Marissa on her hands and knees on a quilt, Evelyn and Will by her side. She wore an oversized T-shirt and socks, but her pants were already off. Rowan crouched next to them, looking like he'd just been slapped.

Marissa's breaths came in short, sharp gasps, and her hands gripped the fabric beneath her. Her chestnut hair was plastered to her forehead, and her eyes were half-closed, her face a mask of concentration and agony.

Kael slowed, approaching warily. Will growled under his breath, his territorial protectiveness and panic warring with his knowledge that he couldn't do this on his own. "Who the hell is this?"

"He's Finn for the moment," Jasper muttered.

Evelyn's hair fell over her shoulder as she leaned in and spoke in calm, soothing tones, instructing Marissa to breathe, to focus on her voice.

Kael took another step, and Will stepped between him and his mate. I waited for Kael to snipe at him, but he didn't. "I know how to deliver pups. I'm going to make sure they're both safe." His voice was calm, authoritative. He didn't wait for a response from Will, just moved past him and dropped to his knees.

Will's dark brown eyes flashed. "How are you going to help with one arm?"

My jaw dropped. Kael didn't answer. He just opened the bag of supplies he'd bought and pulled out a spool of string and scissors. "You've got two choices. I can help as best I can with one arm, or you can deliver this pup yourself."

Will's jaw ticked, and after a moment, he stepped back. "Fine. But if you hurt her—"

"He's not going to hurt her," I snapped. "And that was an

asshole comment." I pushed past him and knelt next to Kael. "How can I help?"

"Let's get her comfortable." He showed me where to put my hands as we helped Marissa into a crouch. He pointed at Will. "I need you to sit behind her and support her so she can relax." Will surprisingly didn't argue. He followed his instructions as Kael unwrapped the string and used his knee to help him cut two lengths, then set them on the blanket.

"I'm going to have Callista take off your underwear so I can see where we're at." Kael looked Marissa in the eyes. Marissa winced in pain and nodded.

I waited for Will to object, but he didn't so much as flinch as I reached under Marissa's shirt and stretched her underwear over her knees. She lifted her heels one at a time.

Kael slipped a towel under her, and it was a good thing he did. Fluid and blood leaked out of her, soaking the fabric. He gave instructions to Rowan and Jasper, then scrubbed his hand with the soap and the bucket of water Bill set next to him.

He dried it on a clean towel and then placed it on Marissa's knee. "I'm going to check to see how close we are to this pup entering the world, okay?"

She nodded once, leaning back on her mate's shoulder. Will whispered something to her, and she nodded, her breathing heavy.

Kael's expression shifted.

"What's wrong?" Will demanded, his voice cracking.

Kael drew a deep breath. "Nothing. Your baby's heart is strong."

He was lying. My heart started to race.

Tell me, I sent to him. With my emotions heightened, it felt as easy as breathing to push my thoughts.

The baby's breech. We need to turn it. Kael moved further up the quilt. "Callista's going to help me turn your baby a bit so he can come out smoothly."

Marissa squeezed her eyes shut. "Okay." She gritted her teeth as another contraction gripped her.

Put your hand on the baby's bottom. Kael put his hand over mine and guided it between Marissa's legs. I held in a gasp as my palm met slick heat. *You're going to apply gentle pressure when I tell you.*

I nodded. He removed his hand and placed his hand on her abdomen.

"Now." Kael began applying pressure with his hand, pushing the baby's head upward, away from the pelvis. I mirrored his movement, my hand on the baby's bottom, applying just enough pressure to assist the turn. Kael guided me with subtle nods and brief instructions, our movements synchronized as if we'd done this a hundred times before.

I felt it again. *Safe.* This version of him, capable and calm—steady—made me want to open my heart wide and drink him in.

"A little more, please." Kael was gentle, and as I adjusted my pressure, the baby started to shift beneath my fingers.

Holy shit. I didn't realize I'd sent that thought until the corner of Kael's mouth twitched. There was the ridge of a spine and then—

"A head. There's a—"

Marissa wailed, bearing down as another contraction hit.

Kael moved back between her knees, and I pulled my hand back. Bill offered me the bucket of water and soap.

Marissa's cries grew more insistent, and Kael breathed with her. "You're doing amazing, Marissa. Just a little longer."

Will's hands shook as he held Marissa's, his knuckles white from the pressure. Evelyn's eyes were wide, her breathing shallow. Kael applied the iodine with gauze, and Rowan was ready next to him with a trash bag.

"On the next contraction, you're going to push, okay?" Kael motioned for Bill to wipe up the mess under her and place another clean towel beneath her and one on Kael's lap.

Marissa let out a guttural moan as she curled into herself, and Kael placed my hands on her knees, showing me how to apply counterpressure.

"Amazing. Breathe deep and then one more like that." His hand was there on the pup's smooth head. Tears pricked my eyes when I saw a shock of dark hair on its tiny head.

"Here we go," Kael soothed as Marissa's body shook with the effort of another push.

Before I could blink, the baby slipped free. Kael caught the newborn, his hand steady as he cradled the tiny, squalling form in his lap.

Will's eyes filled with tears, and he reached out, his hands shaking. "Is it—"

"She's perfect," Kael smiled. He gently wiped the mucous from the baby's face and turned her on her stomach. He didn't have to do anything else. She sucked in a breath and cried. A strong, healthy wail. Kael handed the baby to Marissa, who tucked the pup under her shirt and held her up against her chest, her shoulders shaking with sobs.

Tears trailed over my cheeks. It was the most beautiful thing I'd ever seen.

Kael tapped my hand, handing me the string. "Marissa if you can lower the baby a little." She let her daughter descend, and Kael turned the pup toward us. "Can you tie this there and there?" He pointed to two places on the umbilical cord.

I nodded and did as he asked. "Is that tight enough?"

"Perfect." He reached for the scissors and cut the cord, then looked up at Will. "Help her lean back a little more. Marissa, you're going to feel a few more contractions."

She nodded, and Kael guided her through the final stages of delivering the afterbirth with calm, quiet instructions, never rushing, never letting the intensity of the moment take over. Kael gently coaxed the placenta out and inspected it.

What are you doing? I asked.

I need to make sure it's fully intact. If anything stays inside, it could cause infection.

I wanted to kiss him.

When he was satisfied, Kael moved back off the quilt. He looked up at Will. "You'll need to wash her at home. I don't want her to freeze out here." He turned back to Marissa. "You both did great."

"Thank you," she whispered, clutching the baby to her chest.

Kael reached for the bucket and soap, but Rowan put a hand on his shoulder. Kael looked up. Rowan didn't say anything, just nodded once and stepped back.

I helped clean up, making sure Marissa was comfortable while Kael tended to the final details, saving the afterbirth so she could take it home and dry it. I'd heard in recent years that mundanes had started following our traditions of eating our after birth. Odd since their bodies didn't need the added nutrition of supporting pups who grew at twice the rate of normal humans.

Kael and Bill started packing away the supplies. All of us jumped in to help as Jasper helped Marissa stand. He and Will took a few towels and began to carry her and the pup to their car.

"We'll wash this back at the house," Bill said, telling Evelyn to just toss everything in a trash bag.

Once we'd gathered everything together, we made the trek

back to our trucks. Rowan and Jasper wouldn't let Kael do any of the work. They loaded the supplies and then looked around for anything else that needed doing.

I got in the truck with Lana. Kael walked to the passenger side of Bill's truck, and Rowan strode over to Lana's window.

She rolled it down. "Satisfied?

Rowan lowered his eyes. "Just be safe."

Lana wrapped her hand around the wheel and grinned. "I'm always safe."

Rowan rolled his eyes. He patted the side of the truck then looked up at me. "You and Kael were quite the team."

I wet my lips. "He gave good instructions."

Rowan nodded. "That's the funny thing. I didn't hear half of them." He met my eyes. "But I think you did."

TWENTY-ONE

KAEL

Bill shoved the plate of sandwiches across the table. "Eat."

"I already had one."

He raised an eyebrow. "Have another."

I grunted and took one from the plate.

"Remember the time we found that abandoned cabin up near the Skeena River?" Bill's voice rasped. "Thought we'd struck gold with that stash of canned goods."

I leaned back in my chair. "Until we realized half of them were expired."

Bill chuckled, a deep, rumbling sound that echoed off the walls. "Couldn't tell if it was the spices or the botulism that gave it that kick." He rapped his knuckles on the table. "I don't know why, but being out in the woods today got me thinking about that day."

"It was probably all the blood."

Bill guffawed and dropped his hands to his knees. He let out a long breath. "We may not have been a pack, but we were a family, weren't we?"

I nodded, my throat tightening. We were a family, but it was a family built on a foundation of survival and necessity. Not on the bonds of pack or blood. We were all unanchored.

Bill scratched his beard. "You ever think about it?"

"Think about what?"

"Joining a pack."

I scoffed. "Why would I do that?"

Bill shrugged. "Just a thought."

I gave him a skeptical look. I knew where this was going. "You know why I can't do that. Even if I wanted to."

Bill nodded slowly. "Just because you weren't accepted as a pup doesn't mean you wouldn't be now."

"Drop it, Bill."

His eyes narrowed. "You think you have nothing to offer a mate or a pack? That's a load of shit. You're—"

I stood abruptly, the wooden chair scraping across the floor. "I said drop it, Bill." I took the last bite of my sandwich and walked to the sink to fill a glass with water.

I caught movement at the door and turned. Lana looked between the two of us, and Bill pointed to the plate. "Lunch."

She nodded gratefully and took a seat at the table.

"How's your friend?" Bill asked, and my stomach clenched. Callista had gone straight to her room after we returned to the house.

"She's sleeping." Lana shook her head. "She's dead. It's like she didn't get any sleep last night."

I choked on my water and leaned over the sink. I coughed, trying to clear my lungs. When I recovered, both of them were staring at me.

"Wrong tube?" Bill raised an eyebrow.

My phone buzzed in my pocket, and I pulled it out. My heart sank. *Saved by the literal devil.* "I need to take this."

I strode out the back door, pulling my leather jacket tighter around myself against the chill. The sun was out, but a cold front was blowing in. It would probably storm overnight.

I tensed as I raised the phone to my ear. "Hey."

"Kael."

I breathed a sigh of relief. "Destin." The last time I'd gotten a call like this, it was from one of the alphas.

It was just a call. Destin was just checking in.

The Alliance had been silent for weeks, and now they wanted an update. It was normal. They were just being cautious.

That didn't stop the worry from gnawing at my insides. I knew what they were asking of him. They wanted information, updates, proof that I was still under their thumbs. And if he couldn't provide that, there would be consequences.

"You haven't reported in a while." Destin's breath crackled the speaker.

I walked further into the trees and stopped in front of an oak. "I've had some complications."

Destin lowered his voice as if that would keep them from listening. "They're not patient, Kael. You know that."

I did. All too well. "I should be on to the next target in a couple of days. Let them know if they wanted things to run smoothly, they never should've given the dagger to Nathan Black."

"Right." Destin exhaled. "Okay. I'll pass that on."

The line went dead, and I lowered the phone, my pulse pounding in my ears. I stood there for a moment, staring at the trees, then started back toward the house.

After a couple of steps, I froze. There was a flicker of something through the trees.

I walked faster, my wolf pushing to the surface at the hint of danger, but as I reached Bill's backyard, I didn't catch another glimpse of anything unusual.

With a final look at the trees, I stepped inside and closed the door behind me.

TWENTY-TWO

CALLISTA

I'd slept for barely an hour when my body woke me up to go to the washroom. I was just curling back up in my sheets, trying not to think of how much I wanted Kael back in them when a slight creak made me sit up.

A shadow flickered against the curtains. There was someone outside my window. My heart leaped, but as I rushed forward and pulled the fabric from the glass, the excitement seeped out of me.

Lana dragged herself over the sill and slid to the floor, motioning for me to hurry and shut it.

"What the—"

Lana put a finger to her lips and waved me down next to her. She was breathing hard. "I heard him. Talking to someone on the phone."

"Who?"

She shot me a look. "Who do you think? Kael."

I rubbed my eyes, trying to push through the fog in my brain. "You were eavesdropping?"

She nodded, her expression deadly serious. "I couldn't hear every word, but he was talking about his next target."

I blinked. "What?"

Lana nodded. "He said he'd be out of here in a day or two." A pit opened up in my middle. I swallowed hard. "I don't know who he was talking to."

I bit the inside of my cheek. Had he said that? Why was I surprised? He'd never pretended he wasn't going to continue with whatever job he'd signed up for. He'd only said he wanted to break my bond with the dagger.

Lana watched me, and I straightened. "What?"

"You know what."

I tensed. "No, I don't know—"

"Is he your mate?"

My eyes widened. "How could you even ask that?"

She didn't take the bait. "I heard what Rowan said. Can you speak to him?" She tapped her temple.

My throat was dry. "He thinks it's because of the dagger—"

Lana groaned and dropped her head against the wall. "Why the hell didn't you say something?"

I scoffed. "Here, let me see how that would've gone over." I turned and plastered a smile on my face. "Hey, Lana, you know the guy who tried to slit my throat? I want to bang him."

Lana laughed out loud. "How could anyone argue with that?"

I rolled my eyes and slumped over my knees. "I think we both hope it disappears when we sever the connection with the dagger." My wolf whined, making her dissent known. *Noted.* I patted her head.

Lana looked skeptical. "If there's a bond—"

"There's not a bond." I looked up, resting my chin on my arms. "It's nothing."

She watched me a moment, then nodded. "Okay. Good. Because it sounds like he's moving on." She stood and stretched out her lower back. "It's confusing."

"What is?"

She strode toward the door. "He was so calm today. So good with Marissa. I almost forgot for a moment that he kills for a living."

That pit expanded inside of me as Lana walked out into the hall. I rushed to the washroom and leaned on the counter. *He kills for a living.*

How could I reconcile that with what I'd seen that morning? With how careful he'd been with the baby's head? With how careful he'd been with me...

I splashed water on my face and padded back into the bedroom. I glanced out the window. Clouds were rolling in. Nothing ominous, just gray slowly coating the blue and blocking the sun.

I turned toward the bed, and that's when I saw him. A figure standing at the edge of the yard, half-hidden by the shadows. I frowned. *What was he—*

My throat constricted as he reached for the hem of his shirt. He pulled it over his head and tossed it onto the ground. Just like he had outside the campsite, he took off his pants and boxers and set everything on the ground at the base of a tree.

Kael's body was a work of art, sculpted and powerful, but I couldn't fully appreciate it because my brain was short-circuiting. *What was he doing?* Why was he shifting in the middle of the afternoon? After apparently talking about using the dagger again. Did he just need to blow off some steam?

My blood heated.

Then, before my eyes, his body began to change. His limbs

elongated, his spine curved, and thick fur sprouted from his skin. No matter how many times I'd seen it, shifting still seemed like a dream, surreal and impossible.

As I stared at him, a deep ache settled in my chest. The last time he'd shifted, I hadn't been able to take him in like this. Now he stood against the trees, regal and strong. *Three legs.* After everything he'd done with one hand, I wasn't about to underestimate him like Lana did.

I wanted to run my fingers through his fur, to feel the warmth of his body against mine. My wolf was at attention. *I know, girl.* She wanted to shift so bad, it ached. I looked down at my arm. The wound was nearly healed. Since Lana held the dagger, my skin had been slowly knitting back together, and now all the angry red and oozing was gone.

Kael's wolf form stood still for a moment, his ears twitching. Then, with a flick of his tail, he turned and bounded into the forest. My heart sank as I watched him disappear between the trees, his form swallowed by the darkness.

My wolf pushed so hard against my consciousness I stumbled forward toward the window. *Go,* she pleaded, and with Kael's body fresh in my mind, it didn't take much convincing.

It was my turn to go out the damn window.

I took off my bra and T-shirt, opting for a more easily removable sweatshirt, then opened the pane and lowered myself over the sill.

I kept to the house until I reached the rose bushes, then crouched and ran to the trees. Unlike Kael, I didn't stand where anyone could see me from the house. I moved well into the shadows before pulling off my clothes.

If you're wrong about this, girl, you might not recover.

My wolf growled, impatient. I couldn't blame her. She'd waited too long for his. With a final glance down at my arm, I closed my eyes and let go.

TWENTY-THREE

Kael

I sprinted through the forest, my paws pounding the uneven ground, dodging roots and rocks. The air was cool and crisp, hinting at the rain building in the clouds overhead.

My mind was a whirlwind, torn between the life I once had and the magnetic pull that drew me toward Callista. I used to be free. No links. No responsibilities. I could run, hunt, and live without a second thought.

But in a way, I'd been deluding myself. As much as I sealed myself off from the rest of the shifter world, men like Destin and Bill still mattered to me. It made me vulnerable, and I didn't want more weakness. I already had enough of that to spare.

Then I saw hazel eyes, sparkling with curiosity. The way Callista's nose twitched when she was concentrating hard.

She'd jumped in with that birth, not balking once at the blood and mess. On the one hand, she was everything my old life wasn't. Complicated. Chaotic. On the other? I felt my feet growing roots.

I couldn't have both. Just like I couldn't save both Callista and Destin. But the question was, who would I choose?

My wolf let out a low growl, and I collected the pieces of my situation together again as my lungs burned. *Was there a way?*

Maybe I could use the dagger. The thought slithered through my mind, dark and insidious. I knew its history, knew how it corrupted those who wielded it. Using the dagger to gain the upper hand would lead to nowhere good. It would demand more and more from me until I was lost to its power.

I shook my head, trying to dislodge the idea. No, that wasn't an option. There had to be something else. If Lana succeeded with the dagger, I could try to negotiate with the alphas, and convince them to let Destin go free.

But what would I offer them? My loyalty? No, they already had that on paper. They wouldn't be interested in a token gesture. If anything, they'd want more power, more influence. And I couldn't give them that. Not anymore.

The thought of trying to reason with them made my stomach churn. They were wolves, predators, and anyone who stood in their way was prey. They'd already shown they were willing to use any means necessary to get what they wanted, and I had no reason to believe they'd suddenly play fair.

But what if I could appeal to their sense of self-preservation? Could I convince them that keeping Destin alive and happy would be in their best interest? I could argue that a contented survivalist was more valuable than a resentful one. *Not more valuable than a dead one.*

I had no leverage.

The irony wasn't lost on me. I'd spent years distancing myself from Destin, building a life separate from everyone. Proving I could survive on my own. Now I was faced with the possibility of losing him for good.

But. We didn't know how the magic would work, how it would respond to Lana's offering. I hadn't promised the alphas power. I'd only promised them death.

That sent a shiver down my spine. The idea of slamming down that steel floor, of closing off my humanity like I always did to complete the task in front of me, felt like shackling my feet to the floor.

I'd felt too much these past days. How could I go back to feeling nothing?

I slowed as I neared a clearing, the gray sky making the river look like liquid silver. I paced forward and lowered my head, lapping up the ice-cold water.

I'd come here as a kid. Fished it with Bill. Being around him flooded my head with memories I thought I'd buried. Before Friday night, I was one thing. I was strength and reliability. A get-out-of-jail-free card for the people who hired me.

Now...

Was I a killer? Or was I that six-year-old boy shivering in the trees? Was I a young wolf trying to please whoever he could to make sure he wasn't left out in the cold again? Was I the arrogant asshole that didn't call Destin after he'd left three messages, or was I the man who flew across the world to come home and set him free?

Allowing my wolf to take the lead gave me too much time to think. I was a pressure cooker, with the image of those alphas sitting with their smug faces. A week ago, I didn't care what they wanted as long as Destin walked free.

Now, if I was going to kill anyone...

My muscles twitched, and I shook out my fur. I lowered my head for another drink and froze at the snap of a branch.

I held perfectly still as the wolf emerged from the treeline. She stepped out cautiously, her eyes scanning the area, her fur glinting in the moonlight. Her breath was a steady rhythm, her paws barely making a sound as they pressed into the soft earth of the stream bed.

The she-wolf's fur was a rich russet, her eyes a piercing amber. She moved with a fluid grace, each step deliberate and tense. She paced along the river, her gaze never wavering from the trees on the other side of the shore.

I took a step forward, my breath hitching as she paused. She turned her head, and our eyes locked. The world around us seemed to fade.

For a heartbeat, I forgot everything. The alphas, the dagger, Destin—none of it mattered. I could only focus on the wolf before me and the fire she ignited in my veins.

CHAPTER
TWENTY-FOUR

My mind raced as I paced along the river. Kael. Where the hell was he?

Blake would've been yelling at me for running off into the woods without a plan. He probably wanted to yell at me about a thousand things this weekend. A million more if he knew what Kael and I had been up to in my bedroom. Especially if he knew how much I wanted a repeat performance.

But following him here was more than that. Kael was two opposites in my head, and I needed to know which one was real. How I was going to discover that, I had no idea, but I couldn't sit in my room after what Lana told me. He was running his wolf for a reason, and I wanted to hear it.

My wolf whined in frustration, watching the river gurgle past under the gray sky. Then the wind shifted, and she instantly turned her head. *I smelled it, too, girl.* My heart started to race.

There he was. His coat thick and full, standing next to the river. His eyes locked onto mine as he lowered his head and padded over the soft grass and wildflowers toward me. I waited for him to say something, but when he was a few meters in front of me, he cocked his head to the side, then started to shift.

My wolf seemed confused, but I couldn't look away. The fur on his back rippled, and his eyes, those piercing eyes, stayed locked on mine as his snout shortened and his fur receded. His limbs elongated, and his spine straightened.

And then, there he was. Standing in front of me in all his naked glory. I should've given him some privacy, but I couldn't. I was mesmerized by the transformation, the raw power and grace of it. Why had he done that in front of me? Why was he still standing there?

Kael didn't seem to mind my staring. He didn't move to cover himself. Was he waiting for me?

As if reading my thoughts, a slow smile lifted his mouth, then he turned and strode to the water's edge. As soon as his back was to me, I shifted. My wolf wasn't happy. She'd just gotten to stretch her legs and there I was sending her back again. I mentally inspected her as she settled into my head. She wasn't hurt. I rubbed a hand over the still-raw skin on my arm and breathed a sigh of relief.

Kael waded into the water, and I took a step closer. The clouds were growing darker, making the water nearly black. He walked in up to his waist.

I curled my toes in the grass. "Where are you going?"

He turned back, his eyes traveling up my body. I resisted the urge to wrap my arms around my chest. He'd already seen it. This wasn't anything new.

My body wasn't convinced.

"Going for a swim."

Of course. As you do on a Saturday afternoon after delivering slow pleasure to the woman standing in front of you and, you know, a baby. My pulse quickened as I stepped closer to the water. It was going to be freezing, and the water was already up to his waist.

I dipped my toes in and winced. Ice cold. "Kael—"

He turned back, grinning. "What?"

I gave him a look. "You know what. You're going to get hypothermia in thirty seconds."

"I'll be on the other side in thirty seconds." He watched me. He hadn't asked why I was there or what I wanted, so I didn't question him.

I exhaled and sat down on the bank. "Fine. I'll wait for you."

He smirked and dragged himself back through the water. "Come here."

I pulled my knees closer to my chest. "I don't want to get in."

"I'm aware." He rose out of the water and stood in front of me. My eyes were at waist level, and even though the water was cold—

"My eyes are up here."

I jolted, heat staining my cheeks. Kael laughed as he reached down and tugged on my hand, lifting me from the grass. He squatted, and in one motion, wrapped his arm around my back and scooped my legs from the ground. I gasped and threw my arms around his neck.

He exhaled. "Thanks. That's helpful." Without another word, Kael turned back to the river and walked in.

My eyes widened. "How deep does it get?"

"Not deep enough for you to worry."

I clung to him, watching like a crazy person for any hazards under the surface. If a rock or log popped up, I wouldn't be able to dodge it. "Why do we need to cross this? Couldn't we have talked on the other side?"

"Is that why you're here? To talk?"

I swallowed hard. I didn't know why I was there exactly. Only that it felt like I needed to be. "Yes."

"Talk about what?"

About Lana overhearing your phone conversation. About who you really are and what you want. About this thing between us that I can't stop thinking about. "About what happened this morning."

He grunted as his foot hit a rock. "You did well."

"You gave good instructions."

Kael lifted me higher in his arms as we hit the center of the river. The water barely brushed my butt, and I shivered. He met my eyes. "Good chat."

I shot him a look, but couldn't think of anything else to say as he crossed the final stretch of water and set me down on the bank on the other side.

"Thank you." I rubbed my arms. Even dry, the chill in the air was seeping through my skin.

"You're welcome." He stood in front of me a second longer, his chest and stomach wet and covered in goose flesh, then walked past me up the bank.

I followed, not bothering to ask where we were going. He would either tell me or he wouldn't, but we both knew I was going to follow. Unless there was another frozen river to cross. Despite the cold, my body felt glorious. I took in every tree branch, every late blooming wildflower, every new tree sprouting from the forest floor. I'd missed this. All of it. For nearly a month I'd been stuck in my house staring at a computer screen.

The world was beautiful. And I'd been missing it.

I gritted my teeth to keep the burn in my eyes from turning into tears, but wasn't successful. Tears pooled against my lower eyelids, and I blinked, trying to clear them before Kael turned around.

Then his hand was on my elbow. "Slow down."

I stumbled back and looked at the ground. I'd almost walked right off a ledge. The drop wasn't far, but the rocks were jagged. I quickly wiped my cheeks. "What is this place?"

Kael watched me a moment before clearing his throat. "Hot spring. I found it as a pup." He walked along the edge and dropped into the small semicircular pool.

It wasn't large, and wasn't deep enough to submerge without crunching up, but the water was crystal clear. A vent at the bottom sent ripples through the water, bubbling at the surface.

I bit my lower lip. "This makes me think of that movie."

"Which one?"

"I can't remember the name, but people were skinny dipping in a hot spring and then magma superheated the earth beneath them and they boiled to death."

Kael raised an eyebrow. "Hmm. It's a good thing wolves run hotter than humans." He dropped lower and leaned back against a rock, closing his eyes. "Water's nice. Not boiling."

I rolled my eyes and crouched, slipping in next to him. I exhaled as the sudden heat made my skin tingle, then turned and rested my arms on the rocks, letting my body float. Steam curled around me, sticking to my exposed skin.

I jerked my foot back when something brushed against it.

"Sorry." Kael opened his eyes.

I turned to look at him. "Who were you talking to? When you were on the phone earlier."

His eyes widened a fraction. He straightened in the water. "Were you listening?"

I shook my head. "No. But Lana was."

He nodded once. "My friend. With the alphas."

I considered this. Was there a chance he was telling his friend what he wanted to hear? Was I hoping that's why he'd said what he did? "You have a lot of friends."

Kael scrubbed his hand over his jaw. "I'm lucky, I guess."

"Why don't you have a pack? And why are you willing to do all of this for a 'friend?'"

"Wow, we're just getting right into this."

I leaned closer. "Is killing really such a nothing task to you that you'd knock off a few people anytime, anyplace, or is this more than a friend to you? And you know how to deliver babies? And Bill seems like more than a friend, too, for that matter—"

Kael held up a hand. "You're more talkative than you were last night."

That shut me up. My skin started to flush, and not from the hot spring.

Kael cocked his head. "Why does it matter?"

"Why does *what* matter?"

He shrugged. "Any of it. As soon as we can get to Swan Lake, you hopefully won't be tied to the dagger—"

"So you are going to take it? You're going to use it again?" My shoulders curled in, and I wrapped my arms over my chest.

Kael's jaw worked. "That's the plan."

"Because of your friend. You're going to kill people because of—"

"He was like a father to me. The alphas knew that. I was working over in Europe when I got the call."

I moved to my left and rested against a rock. "Okay. They knew you?"

He nodded. "I grew up about an hour north."

"Which pack?"

His expression darkened, and for a second, I wondered if he wasn't going to answer. "Didn't have one."

I frowned. "Why not."

Kael pointed at his opposite shoulder, watching me as it sank in. My stomach dropped through my middle, and I couldn't keep the look of horror off my face. "Are you serious? They rejected you?"

He dropped his hand back into the water. "Six years old."

My mind reeled. Six. I'd heard of packs ending pregnancies when they didn't think the pups would be strong, but allowing them to live, only to abandon them? "That's horrible."

Kael stared at the water's surface. "Bill thinks my mother tried to keep me. That's why I was so old."

It made sense. She probably suffered just as much as he did. "Which pack?"

"It doesn't matter."

"It does matter. Which pack?" I hadn't meant to growl, but something wild and feral rose within me. How dare they do that to him? How dare they leave him helpless?

Kael put his hand out and pried my clawed fingers from the rock. "I'm fine, Callista."

His touch sent a swoop through me, starting at my wrist and diving into my middle. I pulled back.

Kael cleared his throat. "Destin was like a father to me. He's the one the Alliance got their hands on."

"Alliance?"

Kael looked up. "You don't know about them?" I shook my head. "It's a group of three, maybe four alphas up north. They work together to maintain their packs, share resources, get through the winter. It's tougher up there."

"And they're the ones who hired you." Pieces were starting to click together. "Did you work with Nathan?"

Kael shook his head. "I was just there to clean up his mess."

That stung like a slap. Kael was hired to do what Nathan couldn't. Because he'd tried to kill me, tried to control Evelyn, and Rowan had ripped out his throat. This wasn't a game, and Kael, though he sat relaxed next to me, wasn't innocent. "I'm Nathan's mess," I whispered.

"That's not what I meant."

My eyes flashed. "But it's the truth." He didn't argue, and words bubbled up my throat before I could stop them. "Why didn't you kill me, Kael? In the tent. Why didn't you let me take the dagger and finish what Nathan started?"

"You heard me answer Rowan." Kael pushed up, standing in the water.

"Right. You said you needed to be sure."

"Exactly." He turned and pressed his hand on the rock, readying himself to get out, but I wasn't done with this conversation.

"Why can we talk? In wolf form?"

Kael hoisted himself up onto the rocks. "That's a great question."

"Kael." I struggled up to the bank, storming after him back into the trees. "You don't have any thoughts on that?" He didn't turn. Didn't answer. "Kael—"

He spun and pulled me against his chest, his hand snapping around my waist like a bracelet. "You want to know my thoughts?" His head bowed toward me, his body rock hard against my stomach.

"Mmhmm." I wet my lips, and his eyes turned liquid as he tracked the motion.

"I can't take a mate."

My breath caught as his hips rocked into mine. "I never said I wanted—"

"I don't have a pack. Zero stability. I don't even have a home base."

"Kael, I didn't—"

He brushed his lips over my jaw, and my eyelids closed involuntarily. "I'm sorry," he whispered, then took my hand and walked me to the river.

TWENTY-FIVE

We ran as wolves through the woods in silence. When we got closer to the house, I dropped back and found my clothes. Kael didn't have that option. His were next to the house, and by the time I saw why he shouldn't rush out into the yard, it was too late to stop him.

"Taking a mid-day stroll?" Lana stood next to the back-door, her hands on her hips.

Kael hesitated, then walked to his clothes and started dressing.

"Where is she," Lana barked.

Kael didn't answer, and I rushed to pull on my underwear.

"Answer me, asshole."

"Lana!" I ran out of the trees, my sweatshirt on, but no pants. "Stop. It's not what it looks like."

"Yeah? What does it look like, do you think?"

I shoved my feet through the leg holes and pulled up my pants. "It *looks* like we were mating in the trees." I panted. "But we weren't."

My response took her off guard. She glowered at the two of us. "What were you doing then? Alone. And *naked*."

"I shifted, Lana." I straightened, tossing my hair behind my shoulder. "My wolf was fine."

Lana ground her teeth. "And you expect me to believe he just stood there? Didn't even notice you were still in heat?"

Kael's jaw tightened. "I don't give a shit what you believe."

Lana's eyes flashed. "You think you can just do whatever you want, don't you?" She took a step closer to him, her arms tensing. "You think you can come into our territory, threaten our pack, and then—"

"Nothing happened," I blurted out. Which was technically true. Even though my heart felt like it had an ice pick jabbed in the middle of it. "I was trying—"

"Just stop." Lana cut me off, her eyes boring into mine. "I don't care what you were or weren't doing. What I care about is that he thinks he can waltz in here and disrupt everything." She turned back to Kael, her voice dripping with disdain. "You're not even part of a pack. You don't get to break our rules."

Kael's eyes darkened, and my stomach twisted. "Lana, stop."

"You're trying to what? Prove something?" Lana scoffed. "You've already proven you can't be trusted. That you're a threat."

I gaped at her. What was she talking about? She hadn't said a word of this to me, and now she was acting like this?

Lana pointed a finger at him, her eyes blazing. "And if you think for one second that I'm going to let you—"

"Enough!" Kael's voice thundered against the house, and I jumped. He took a step forward. Kael straightened his T-shirt. "You don't get to tell me what I can and can't do."

Lana's eyes narrowed. "This is our territory—"

"Like hell it is. This is neutral land."

Lana ground her teeth. "We're only here because you forced us—"

"I forced her." Kael pointed at me. "You're here by choice."

Lana's hands shook with rage. "I'm third in command of the Black Lake Pack. I can tell you whatever the hell I want."

Kael's eyes darkened, his breath coming in shallow bursts. "I'm not part of your pack. Remember?"

Lana's nostrils flared as Kael stalked past her up the steps. He walked into the house and slammed the door.

Before I could catch my breath, Bill stumbled out onto the porch holding his shotgun. "You girls okay?"

"I could've used that a second ago," Lana muttered.

Bill looked back at the house. "For what?"

Lana huffed a breath. "I'm done with this." She stormed past me into the trees.

We had to leave. If Kael and Lana had to spend another night trapped in this house, they were going to combust, and my heat, though still uncomfortable, was manageable.

"All that commotion was the two of them?" Bill pointed between the house and the trees.

"It's not like her," I said.

Bill scratched his beard. "It's not like him. But, then again..." He fixed his eyes on me.

"What?" I crossed my arms.

"Nothing. Just thinking."

I shoved my hands in my pockets and walked to the steps. I wanted to rush in after Kael and apologize for what Lana had said. *You're not even part of a pack.*

Something wasn't right. I hadn't known Lana for long, but she hadn't been cruel even when Kael had a knife to my throat. "I don't think we can wait any longer. We need to leave for Swan Lake."

I SAT ON MY BED, threading my thoughts between that afternoon with Kael and my worries about what we might find at the pools.

I wanted him. I wanted to be safe. I wanted him to give up the dagger. I wanted to go back to my normal life. I wanted...

There was no easy answer. After tonight, I would hopefully be free of my wound. But despite all the reasons why I should want to be free of Kael, I couldn't make it sink into my heart.

I ran my hands through my hair, then padded down the hall to the bathroom. I washed my face and brushed my teeth, then walked into the hall. The door to Lana's room was open. She was stuffing her duffle bag.

I leaned against the doorframe. "Hey."

She looked up, her eyes rimmed with red. "Hey."

"We should probably get moving. Bill said it was a bit of a drive to the lake."

Lana nodded. "I'll be ready in a minute."

I left her to it and headed back to my room to grab my own things. When I was packed, I walked out to the living room where Kael and Bill were waiting.

"Ready to go?" Bill asked.

I nodded, trying to keep my eyes from sliding to Kael. "Yeah, just waiting for Lana."

Bill grunted. "She's probably packing up her emotions. Those are harder to fold."

Kael's lip twitched.

I turned toward the door. "She's fine. Just tired."

"Seems to be going around." Bill gave Kael a sidelong glance. I searched for my boots.

Lana emerged from the hall with her bag slung over her shoulder. "Ready."

We all filed out the door and got into the trucks. Bill and Kael in one, Lana and I in the other. I buckled my seatbelt and glanced at Lana. "You good to drive?"

She nodded. "Yeah, I'm good."

I settled back in my seat. My thoughts were so thick, I couldn't wade through them to find a superficial bit of conversation. Instead I wandered through everything I'd learned over the past two days.

One weekend. It was laughable how different it had been compared to how I'd envisioned it. How much better.

"Thank you," I whispered.

Lana scoffed. "For what?"

"For holding the dagger. For making me feel so much better."

Lana clenched the wheel. "It wasn't hard."

"Well, I'm grateful."

She nodded once, and we slipped back into silence. The trees blurred by. The drive to Swan Lake was winding, and I had to train my eyes straight out the windshield to keep from getting woozy.

After we passed a small sign that announced ten kilometers to Swan Lake, I turned to Lana. My mouth opened and closed. Her fingers were clenched on the steering wheel, her hands at ten and two. Her eyes were glassy, and she clenched her teeth.

"Lana—"

"I don't feel well."

I searched for the water bottle I'd put on the floor. "Here, let me—"

"No, Callista, I think something's wrong."

I held out the water. "Are you sick?"

Lana didn't answer. She followed Kael's truck onto a narrow road that led up a hill through dense forest. The trees were so thick, they created a canopy over the gravel road. "It's hard to breathe in here."

I frowned. "Do you want to pull over and get some fresh air?"

"No. I want to get to the lake." She shot me an irritated look.

My heart started to pound. *This wasn't like her.* My eyes dropped to her waist where the dagger sat. "I think we should pull over."

Lana's breathing grew more labored. "No, I don't want to stop. I just need to—" She winced, and I reached for her arm.

"Lana, what—"

She gasped, and her hand wrapped around the dagger's hilt through her shirt. "I don't know!"

"Let's pull over, Lana. Put your foot on the brake."

Lana's voice shook. "We're almost there."

I reached out, but before I could touch her, she let out a guttural growl and the car swerved off the road.

TWENTY-SIX

KAEL

Everything happened in a split second. One moment, Callista and Lana's truck was behind us, the next, it was screeching off the road, tires skidding on gravel.

"What the hell—" My words were drowned out by the hiss of brakes. The truck plowed into the underbrush, kicking up a cloud of dust and needles.

"Kael, watch out!" Bill gripped the dash.

I swerved, barely avoiding a collision with a motorbike in the opposite lane and slammed on the brakes. My heartbeat thundered in my ears, my breath catching in my throat.

Bill sat next to me, his eyes wide. "What in the name of—"

I didn't wait for him to finish. My door was open before the truck had fully stopped, and I was out, sprinting back down the road. My eyes scanned the scene, my brain trying to make sense of what I was seeing. The truck was half-buried in the underbrush.

"Kael, wait!" Bill's voice was a distant echo.

I didn't wait. I couldn't. *Callista.* My thoughts were a jumbled mess, but one thing was clear—I had to get to her. Had to make sure she was okay.

The smell of burning rubber filled my nostrils as I ran. Bill's boots pounded behind me.

"Shit." I sprinted as soon as I saw black fur against the driver's window. "She shifted!" I called out to Bill. How had Lana shifted while driving? My hand was on the door handle when I heard the screams.

The dagger. Lana had been holding the dagger. If she shifted, it would've dropped.

I rounded the front of the truck. "Open the door for her!"

I made it before he did. I yanked the door open, and Lana snapped at me, her nails digging into the console as she tried to force me back.

"Lana, it's me!" I held up my hand. "I'm trying to help her."

Lana's wolf growled low in her throat. I moved forward, reaching for Callista, but as soon as I got close, Lana lunged, her teeth snapping inches from my hand.

I stumbled back, my heart racing. "Shit. Okay, okay." I bowed my head, trying to show I wasn't a threat. "I'm not going to hurt her."

Bill finally did as I asked, giving Lana's wolf an easy path off the driver's seat. Her seat was torn up, and Callista was curled around her seatbelt, moaning.

Bill whistled, finally getting Lana's attention.

As soon as she turned, I leaned in. "Hey." I cupped her jaw in my hand and lifted her head. Her eyes were squeezed shut, and she gasped for breath. I saw the blood next. Not on her head, but soaking the arm of her shirt.

"Kael, a little help—" Bill yelled and stumbled back from the door. Lana snarled, her hackles raised.

"It's the dagger," Callista gasped. "It's affecting her. She's been off since this morning, and the closer we got to Swan Lake, the worse she was."

"Why didn't you call?"

Callista struggled to unbuckle her seat belt. "I don't have your number!"

I blinked, then reached over her and hit the red button, then pulled her out of the truck. Of course she didn't have my number. Bill didn't even have my number. But the idea that she couldn't contact me felt strange and...wrong.

"I didn't have time—I couldn't think to push a thought—"

"You have first aid in your bag?" I asked.

Callista nodded, and I looked up to see the dark fur of Lana's wolf gone. She'd shifted back and leaned against the other side of the vehicle. Bill stood with his back to me, giving her privacy.

I pulled Callista's bag from the back and tore through it until I found her supplies. Plenty of gauze. She'd come prepared.

I helped her take off her shirt and wrapped the wound to keep the blood from soaking anything else. It wasn't proper wound care, but it would do for now.

"Shh." I ran my hand over her hair and pulled her to my chest. "I'm so sorry." I wanted to scream at Lana to hurry the hell up, but I kept my mouth shut.

Lana's hands trembled as she searched in the bed of the truck. She dragged a tub over the corrugated metal and pulled out an extra pair of clothes. As soon as she was dressed, she scrambled into the cab and found the dagger on the floor.

Callista's body drooped as she caught her breath.

Lana stood in the brush. Her face was pale, her lips bloodless. "I don't know what happened. I didn't mean to shift, I just—"

"It's the curse." Callista's voice was hoarse. "I think it's affecting you. We have to get to the pools."

Lana shook her head, her hands shaking. "No, we need to go back. We need to get you to a healer."

Callista's grip on my arm tightened. "No, we—"

"I don't give a shit what you want." Lana said, then turned on me, her eyes blazing. "You just want your boyfriend to get to the pools so he can complete his mission."

I frowned. "Lana, that's not—"

"Don't lie to me. I heard everything."

Anger flared in my chest.

She leaned into the truck. "You're just using us. Using Callista to get to your precious relic and finish your mission." She took a step closer. "You think I can't see what you're doing? Trying to endear yourself so you have easier access to kill. To go after whoever you think deserves it."

"It's the dagger," Callista hissed. "This isn't Lana talking."

My fist clenched, and I had to force myself to stay still.

"Get in the truck." Lana nodded at Callista.

I scoffed. "Hell, no." Lana's eyes flashed, but I didn't give her the chance to get in another dig. "Callista's driving with us. If you want to help your friend, you'll have to get this hunk of metal out of the mud and follow."

TWENTY-SEVEN

I gripped the truck seat, not sure if I was trying to ground myself or keep from jumping out of the moving vehicle. Beside me, Bill leaned against the door, his grizzled beard brushing his chest. Kael sat on the other side of the bench seat.

The sides of our thighs touched, and as much as I tried to tell myself it meant nothing, my heart still beat faster. *I can't take a mate.* He'd made himself extremely clear. But he still came for me. He still took care of me. He hadn't gone to Lana first.

Lana. I couldn't stop thinking about her. She'd been there with me through everything, and now she was in her truck by herself. Alone and dealing with . . . well, whatever this was.

Kael had been smart to force her hand. Lana wasn't in her

right mind, and I couldn't predict what she would've done. Taken me back to Bill's? Back to Black Lake?

The truck hit a pothole, and I bounced in my seat, my hip pressing against Kael's. I sucked in a breath and pulled away, but my wolf didn't. She whined, wanting to press closer. She was confused. Frustrated. It had only taken a few minutes in the truck with Kael for her to start running circles in my head.

I couldn't pretend this was just heat or lust or dark magic from the dagger anymore. Yes, Kael was dangerously hot, and it was normal to have a physical reaction to someone like him. I'd heard enough stories about mating bonds to understand how they could skew your perspective, but what I felt around Kael wasn't that either.

It was his heart. His energy. There was no other way to describe it. It was like being on the beach, closing my eyes, and feeling the power of the waves as they crashed against the shore. I couldn't see the force of them, but I could feel it. Like a pulse, a heartbeat.

I was attuned to his scent, even when he masked it, I noticed. I was tuned to his frequency. And he couldn't take a mate.

It was good, wasn't it? I didn't trust myself to make the right choice where he was concerned. Everything he'd whispered to me on the river bank was true. He didn't have a pack or any stability. Wasn't that what I wanted? A safe place to live? A place to raise pups?

That thought only made me think about Kael delivering Marissa's baby, which wasn't helping. I shifted in my seat and tried to focus on something else. Anything.

But the movement of the truck kept jostling me, forcing me to touch him. Every accidental brush sent my wolf into a low-grade frenzy. She craved him. With every bump, it was like she was trying to climb out of my skin and into his.

It's not going to happen, I soothed, trying to help her settle. When she insisted that Kael was our home, I sent a picture of our house, my bedroom. When she said that Kael was safety, I brought to mind my alpha, my brother, and Jasper. She growled, stamping her paws.

What was she trying to tell me? Kael was a rogue wolf. Why was she—?

I jolted as if someone had thrown a bucket of ice water over my head.

"You're an alpha," I blurted.

Kael's eyes snapped to mine. "What?"

I sucked in a breath, then exhaled with a laugh. "You're a damn alpha, that—" I pressed my hands on the dash. That made so much sense. No wonder my wolf was so drawn to him. It *was* his energy, just not in the way I thought.

"Hot damn. She figured it out before you did." Bill's eyes glinted with amusement.

I turned to him. "Did you know?"

Kael sat back in his seat, shifting his eyes out the window. "There's nothing to figure out. It doesn't matter."

Bill scoffed. "It matters. You just don't want it to."

Kael's jaw tensed. "I don't have a pack. I don't *want* a pack."

"That's not what I asked." I leaned forward.

Kael looked over at me, his eyes dark. "I wondered if I was."

I thought about him standing up to Rowan in the woods. Then again in Bill's living room. He'd held his own with Lana and Jasper, which was no small feat. "When? How did you find out?"

Kael shrugged. "When I was young."

"How young?" I couldn't pull my eyes away from his.

"I don't know. Ten? Eleven?"

"And you just . . . ignored it?" I asked. "You felt the draw to lead, and you walked away from it?"

Kael's eyes narrowed. "I never said I felt the draw to lead."

"Then what—"

"I don't want to lead anyone." Kael's voice was low and rough. "I'm not fit to lead anyone."

Bill grunted. "You know, the ones who think that are usually the best leaders."

Kael's eyes snapped to the road, his hand tightening on the wheel. "Not interested."

"Destin would be proud," Bill murmured.

Kael's nostrils flared. "Destin taught me to survive on my own."

Bill stroked his beard. "Parents always teach what they know. It doesn't mean they want you to stop there."

"Still not good enough, then." Kael's expression was hard. There was a long silence, the only sound the rumble of the truck's engine and the crunch of gravel under the tires.

Bill finally broke the silence as we slowed, closing in on the turn off for the pools. "You think leading is about being good enough? About not making mistakes?"

Kael didn't respond, his eyes fixed on the road.

Bill shook his head. "Leading is about caring. About putting others first. You know how to do that. You always have."

Kael's jaw clenched. "Packs are focused on strength and safety. And they'll do whatever it takes to get it."

"You think that's all packs are about?" I asked, my voice barely above a whisper. "Sacrifice and power?" Kael's eyes flicked to mine, and I looked down at my hands. "Maybe it is for some. But the pack I grew up in? It was about family. About loyalty. Protection. Not just for ourselves. For the wolves and humans—"

"That's a nice dream."

I pursed my lips. It suddenly felt imperative that he understand there were other options. "It's not just a dream. You find what you look for."

We turned off the main road and onto a narrow path. The truck bounced as Kael navigated the rough terrain. We passed through a dense stand of trees, their branches unkempt. Kale pulled into a makeshift parking spot at the end of the path.

We got out of the truck as Lana pulled in next to us. I waited in front of the truck, watching as she opened her door, not sure which Lana she'd be this close to the pools. I pressed a hand over my arm. It had stopped bleeding the second Lana picked the dagger back up, but who knew if she was going to keep it.

She walked past us, not saying a word as she headed toward the pools. Steam rose in curling tendrils, just like it had the other night next to the river. Unlike the woods near Bill's house, though, this air felt thick. Heavy. *Magic.*

The word whispered through my mind, and my skin prickled. I took a few more steps until I was fully in the clearing. This place was alive. I hadn't been lucid the last time I was here. I'd missed all of this.

My wolf paced within me, her ears perked and her nose twitching. She felt it too, the pulse of energy that thrummed just below the surface. Something that made my heart race and my skin tingle. It was familiar, yet foreign. Comforting, yet terrifying.

My memories were shards of glass, each piece reflecting a different part of that night Nathan had used me as bait. I remembered the feel of the restraints, the cold bite of metal against my skin.

But there were other things, too. Things I couldn't quite grasp. The scent of wet earth, the hiss of steam. The way the air had seemed to shimmer, like I was looking through a pane of frosted glass.

I took a step forward, then another, drawn to the pool like a moth to a flame. The warmth enveloped me, seeping into my bones and coaxing me to relax. My wolf whined, and I knew she felt it too. The pull. The promise of something more.

Kael's hand shot out, gripping my arm. "Careful."

I looked up at him, my wolf pushing against my skin, urging me to get closer. "I have to see it."

He hesitated, then nodded. "Alright. But stay close."

I nodded, and we moved together, Bill following a few steps behind. As we rounded the shed, the pool came into view. It was larger than I'd imagined, the water a deep, clear blue that seemed to glow in the dim light. Steam rose from the surface in thick, swirling clouds, and the ground around the pool was a mix of wet earth and smooth, slick rocks.

I stopped at the edge, my breath catching in my throat. Lana was already there. She'd stripped off her coat and rolled up her sleeves, revealing her bare arms. Her breath came in quick, shallow gasps, and her eyes were wild. She lay down on her stomach and draped her arms over the side, dipping her arms into the pool. The water lapped at her skin, beads of moisture forming and then slipping back into the depths.

"Lana," I called out. I wanted her to look at me. To let me know that she knew what she was doing.

She didn't respond, her focus entirely on the water that now covered her elbows. The heat was oppressive, the steam making it hard to breathe. I took a step closer, but Kael's hand shot out, grabbing my arm.

"Wait."

Lana moved, and I snapped back to reality. She pulled her arms out of the water, her skin glistening, and reached for the dagger. My breath caught in my throat as she gripped the hilt, her knuckles white.

"Lana, you don't have to—" I started, but the words died in my throat as she raised the dagger.

Time seemed to slow. The metal blade gleamed in the dim light, and I could see the intricate designs etched into the hilt. Symbols I didn't recognize, but that felt ancient and powerful. Lana's hand shook as she held the dagger over her arm, the tip hovering just above her skin.

I wanted to look away, but I couldn't. Her eyes finally met mine, and in that instant, I saw her. The real her. Not the desperate woman in the truck, but the strong, determined wolf who'd launched at Kael in the tent.

She looked down, and with a swift motion, she drew the blade across her forearm. Blood welled up, dark and crimson, and dripped into the pool. The water hissed as it made contact, steam rising in thick plumes.

Lana's breath hitched, and she bit her lip, her face contorting in pain. But she didn't stop. She drew the blade across her other arm, then thrust both forearms back into the water.

The air seemed to hum with energy, the steam swirling in frantic patterns. I took a step forward, but Kael's grip tightened. "Wait," he repeated, his voice a low growl.

The power built, a pressure against my skin that made my ears ring. The water in the pool started to bubble, the surface churning as if something massive moved beneath it. Lana's eyes widened, and she let out a strangled gasp. Her back arched, and the dagger slipped from her grasp, clattering to the rocks. She tried to pull her arms out of the water, but they were stuck, her muscles straining against an invisible force.

The ground trembled, and I stumbled, Kael's arm the only thing keeping me upright. The steam thickened, and the air grew so hot it was hard to breathe. My blood pounded in my ears, and my wolf howled within me, urging me to bolt.

"Lana!" I shouted, but my voice was swallowed by the roar of the water.

Then it happened. The pressure reached a breaking point, and with a deafening crack, energy exploded. I was thrown backward as the shockwave hit me. The world spun, and I landed hard on my back, the air knocked from my lungs.

When my vision cleared, I immediately looked for Kael. What I found made the blood in my veins turn to ice. Lana strode toward me, her eyes wild, her hand gripping the dagger. The runes on the hilt glowed a ghostly white.

This wasn't my friend anymore.

This was my executioner.

CHAPTER
TWENTY-EIGHT

KAEL

I barely had time to process Lana's movement before I was sprinting. When she lunged for Callista, every thought in my head disappeared.

Protect.

Nothing else mattered. Not Bill, not the dagger, not Destin or the alphas. What had gone wrong? One moment Lana was making the blood sacrifice, and the next, she was hunting Callista down.

I was a blur, moving almost faster than I could process. My vision narrowed to a pinpoint focus on my target. I slammed into Lana, and we both went down. Lana hit the ground hard, and the dagger slipped from her grasp. It dropped to the grass.

"Ah!" Callista doubled over, clutching her arm.

The dagger.

My muscles tensed, and I shoved off the floor. I had to get

to it before Lana. Even Bill's voice yelling at me to stop was only a buzz in the background. I didn't care what it did to me or what had happened in that pool.

My fingers were inches away when Lana swooped to grab it. I collided with her, sending her sprawling, but she gripped the hilt in her fingers.

"Lana, look at me! Look at me!" I tightened my grip on her leg as she writhed beneath me, her eyes wild. She thrashed, her foot connecting with my chest. I grunted but held firm. "Lana!"

Her eyes flicked to mine, and there was a glimmer of recognition. Then her expression hardened, cold and detached. I knew that feeling well.

"Kael!" Bill called out. "She can't fight it!"

"No shit!" I growled as Lana twisted, catching my jaw with her boot. She was stronger than she should've been. I scrambled to get a hold on her, but the fabric of her pants tore as she ripped herself out of my grip.

She rose, spinning, and as she lifted her hand above her head, I caught the shift of her grip on the dagger. Lana was going to throw it.

This time, I didn't bolt for her, I lunged for Callista. "Get down!" She turned to me with wide eyes, her lips parted in surprise.

There wasn't time. The dagger left Lana's hand, and I dove in front of Callista. I threw my arms around her, curling her into my chest and bracing for the blade to sink into the muscles of my back.

But it never came.

Something hard knocked into me, and Callista and I were falling.

CHAPTER
TWENTY-NINE

CALLISTA

My head was spinning. I blinked, trying to piece together what had just happened. I was sprawled on the ground with Kael caging me against the ground. The cool, damp earth pressed against my back.

Where was Lana? She was there. The dagger in her hand.

"Kael." I struggled to push myself up onto my elbows, and he lifted his weight from my chest, still positioning himself between me and any oncoming danger.

I gasped when I saw him. Bill. His grizzled form was crumpled on the forest floor. "No —"

Kael was already moving, whirling and grabbing onto Bill's shoulders. "Bill!" His voice cracked, and my heart wrenched in my chest.

The hilt of the dagger protruded from his chest. Directly

over his heart. I searched for Lana and found her a few feet away, her face in the dirt.

What the hell had happened?

"Bill," Kael pleaded, lifting the man's head and shoulders into his lap.

I didn't know what to do. This wasn't like the birth where I could jump in and take direction. Bill's face was ashen, his chest spasming.

A tingling sensation started at my core and spread outward, like sinking into a hot bath after a winter hike. My hand flew to my arm, feeling for my wound. But there was nothing. Just smooth, unbroken skin. My hand trembled as I ran my fingers over the spot, disbelief warring with relief. All of it was followed by a pit opening up in my stomach. If my wound was gone, that meant—

A gurgling sound pulled my attention back to Bill. Blood pooled around him, soaking into the forest floor. Kael's hand pressed uselessly against the wound. Lana pushed up from the ground, wiping the dirt from her cheeks.

Blood. The dagger had taken his blood. But how was it possible?

Kael pressed his hand against Bill's cheek. "Why did you do this?" He knelt in the pooling blood, his fingers trembling. "Why would you—"

Bill's eyes flicked to his, and he smiled. "Kael . . ." His voice was barely a whisper. "You know why."

The forest seemed to hold its breath. The dappled sunlight filtering through the trees cast a warm, golden glow on Bill's face, making him look like an angel.

Kael shook his head, and Bill's hand reached up to rest on Kael's arm. "It's okay, pup. It's okay." His eyes closed for a moment.

Lana watched on in disbelief. She was shaking, tears streaming down her face. "It accepted him but not me."

I shook my head, confused. "What do you mean?"

Lana squeezed her eyes shut. "Something went wrong. When it touched my blood, it didn't accept it. The dark power surged through it—surged into me."

I swallowed hard, my throat dry. Lana's blood was supposed to satiate the dagger, not provide a more deadly vehicle. But what did we know? We'd based our plan on an elementary understanding of the relics. Of course we'd misunderstood the power it held. The link that Lana had with the Shadow Pack.

Lana crawled forward, tears spilling down her cheeks. "Why didn't you tell us?" She stared directly at Bill.

Bill's eyelids shuttered. His breath coming in quick bursts.

Lana's eyes locked onto mine. "When the dagger touched me, I saw things. Memories that weren't mine. A pack, the Shadow Pack." Her voice wavered. "I saw them before the curse, before the relics. And I can see him now. I can see his wolf."

I stared at her, my mind racing. "Bill. He's Shadow Pack?"

Lana nodded, her hands pulled into fists. "The dagger wasn't satisfied with a taste. It still required a life. If I had given more—"

Bill coughed, and Lana's head jerked up. She scrambled to his side, her hands hovering over him. "I'm sorry. I'm so sorry."

Bill turned his head to look at her, his eyes glassy. "It's not your fault, Lana."

She shook her head, and a sob broke free of her lips.

Bill reached up and grabbed her hand. "This was my fate." His voice was hoarse, barely more than a whisper. "You have to fulfill the legends. You need to reunite the pack." Bill's grip on her hand tightened. "The Shadow Pack. It's the only way the packs will be strong again. The only way to protect what's coming."

Lana paled. "What's coming?"

Bill's eyes fluttered closed. "You have to find the others, Lana. You have to—" His grip weakened, and his hand fell to Kael's lap.

Lana's breath came in ragged gasps as she watched the life drain from his eyes. "Bill, please. Please don't go."

He didn't respond. His eyes were vacant. His chest still.

THIRTY

Lana swiped at her cheeks as she pushed up from the grass.

Kael cleared his throat. "Lana—"

"Don't." Her fingers trembled as she pulled her phone from her pocket and swiped open the screen. She stalked into the trees, and I followed. She didn't seem like she wanted moral support, but she was shaking like a leaf.

I glanced back at Kael. He'd shifted so Bill's body was flat on the ground. He was already starting to fade. There was never a need for a burial with shifters. The earth knew where we came from and was eager to take us back.

"Rowan?" Lana sniffed, and I turned, trying to give her space but keep her in my line of sight. "She's fine. Yes, I'm fine."

I could only imagine Rowan's anxiety with all this. It had

been a leap of faith for him to give the task over to Lana. He never would've done it had he not had a new mother and pup to care for.

Lana paced. "It's done." She paused. "I don't know, but it's not going after her. The wound is healed." She glanced up at my arm. I waited as she listened and nodded, then finally hung up the phone.

"Let's go." Lana's shoulders were tense as we turned and strode back to the pools. The second we left the trees, my heart sank.

"What the hell?" Lana growled.

The dagger was gone. *Kael was gone.*

Images of him flashed in my mind. His intense, stormy eyes. The way his lips curved when he smirked. The heat of his body pressed against mine. I could still feel his touch, still hear his voice.

I gritted my teeth and ran forward, searching the grass. "You didn't take the dagger?"

Lana shook her head. "I couldn't touch it. After—"

"Kael took it, Lana!" I pointed where Bill's clothes lay in a heap. I wrapped my arms around myself, trying to keep my heart from shattering.

Lana cursed under her breath. "Why didn't you grab it?"

"Are you kidding me right now?" I snapped.

"You're wound is healed, isn't it?" Lana pointed at my arm.

I rubbed my temples. We shouldn't be fighting. It wasn't either of our fault that Kael had done what he'd said he was going to do all along. "He said he wanted to break the bond. We did. Of course he left."

Lana watched me, and I worked to keep tears from filling my eyes. I'd been so stupid. Of course Kael had left. He didn't want me, he didn't want anyone. He worked alone, and no flash of a mating bond was going to change that.

Lana's expression hardened. "We have to get back to Black Lake. Rowan will need to put out a warning to the other packs—"

"About Kael?" My throat burned.

Lana's eyes flared. "Yes, about Kael."

Pressure built behind my eyes as I imagined Kael stalking other wolves. "He won't do it."

Lana scoffed. "He just walked away with the most dangerous weapon in existence, Callista. And you think he's not dangerous? You think he's not going to use it again?"

I shook my head. "He wouldn't. He—"

"He what? He wouldn't kill another pack member? He wouldn't use that thing against you? Because I'm pretty sure he already did."

I opened my mouth, but the words died on my tongue. He wouldn't harm someone unless it was to protect. But that's what he was doing, wasn't he? He'd found a way to avoid hurting me, but the alphas still held his friend. The closest thing to a father he'd ever had.

Lana's expression softened. "Callista, I know you want to see the best in him—"

"No, you're right." I struggled to breathe. "If Kael kills, the dagger gets more powerful. If the dagger gets more powerful, then the alpha alliance gets more powerful. They're the ones who are creating this bloodbath, and they're the ones who are going to win if we don't stop them."

Lana blinked.

I ran a hand through my hair. "He doesn't have a choice, Lana. They have him in a vice. They tell him who to kill, and he does it or his only family dies. He doesn't have a pack. He doesn't have anyone to back him up." I blew out a breath. "If they had Blake, I'd probably do the same thing."

"Who the hell is 'they?'" Lana's arms crossed over her chest.

My cheeks warmed. *Right.* I hadn't told her about this. About any of it. "You remember that phone conversation you overheard?"

Lana nodded. Why hadn't I told her about it? Right. Because she'd gotten into a yelling match with Kael the second we got back to the house.

I ignored that detail and continued. "Kael told me about the alpha alliance. They hired Nathan, then took someone Kael cares about to force him to come back and clean up the mess. They're forcing him to do this. To kill wolves from other packs and feed their power into that dagger."

Lana stared at me, her eyes searching my face. "You knew this, and—"

"I didn't have time, Lana! You didn't exactly want to chat in the truck on the way here!" It was a low blow. It wasn't her fault the dagger had been affecting her. "I'm sorry—"

"No. You're right." Lana's brow furrowed. She pursed her lips, then finally nodded. "Let's go talk to Rowan."

I let out a shaky breath. As we started back through the forest, my mind raced. I had to get to Rowan. We wanted to figure out a way to stop Kael from killing, to free him from the Alliance.

But Kael had made it clear he didn't want my help. He didn't want my attachment. What was I supposed to do with that?

I slid into the passenger seat and rubbed my arm. Clean. Healed. I could go back to normal life, now. I wasn't part of pack leadership. I didn't need to worry about the Alliance or the dangers they posed to the British Columbia packs. I could go back to my regular life if I wanted to.

Work. Friends. Family. Wasn't that what I wanted?

The sun dropped low on the horizon as we raced down the gravel road. There was an empty pit in my center, but no matter how deep my breaths, it never seemed to fill.

Kael had made his choice. He'd taken the dagger and left me behind. Just like he said he would.

I can't take a mate.

I pressed my hand to my chest, clutching the fabric of my shirt. It would fade, wouldn't it? This bond I felt with him?

Tears pricked my eyes because I didn't want it to. He was a rogue alpha. A rejected wolf. He had no pack, no home base.

None of it mattered to me. He was good. He was kind. He was strong.

My wolf pawed at the ground, pressing against my mind with urgency. *You weren't wrong. About any of it,* I whispered.

She yipped, and, though I didn't think it was going to make any difference, I let her do it her way one last time.

THIRTY-ONE

Kael

I gripped the steering wheel, the leather cracked and worn beneath my palms. My truck rumbled like a beast beneath me down the gravel roads.

I couldn't lose another friend. Not after Bill. The thought of Destin alone in whatever hell hole the Alliance was holding him in twisted my insides. I had to save him.

I glanced at the dagger in the passenger seat. Would it still work? My jaw worked as I sorted through all the possibilities. I could take it back. Tell them what happened and explain about the Shadow Pack.

That would likely require me to give Lana's name. Possibly not. I could give them Bill's. He was gone so at least they couldn't hurt him like they could Lana. But would they release Destin for information? Or would they force me into a task that was worse?

My mind drifted to the price I'd have to pay. The things they could make me do to get him out of there. My grip tightened on the wheel. I wasn't a stranger to violence. To death. But now it was different.

If I didn't take the dagger back, I'd would have to kill two pack members to save Destin.

The thought settled like a stone in my gut. I'd have to rip their throats out. Two men who had probably done nothing but protect their pack. Two shifters who had mothers and fathers and possibly mates. Did they have pups? My stomach churned at the thought of them waiting for their fathers to come home, only to be told they never would.

I passed a small town, its wooden buildings weathered and worn. A couple of cars were parked outside a diner, and a few people walked along the sidewalk. It was a simple life, one that I'd never known. One that I'd never wanted. Until now.

I shook my head, trying to clear my thoughts, but my mind wandered back to holding Callista against my chest. To feeling her lips on my skin. To the sound of her quickened breathing as I touched her.

Then to hovering in Callista's tent. I could feel the fabric between my fingers as I pulled it aside. The way the moonlight had shifted, illuminating her sleeping face. She'd looked peaceful, oblivious to the world outside. Oblivious to me standing there, ready to take her life.

I skidded to a stop on the side of the road and threw open the door of my truck, then stumbled into the ditch and threw up in the grass. My heart beat in my throat. My hands were cold and clammy.

I was a different breed of monster, now. Try as I might, I couldn't get myself to that cold, dead place I used to go to. Not after holding Bill in my arms. Not after Callista said I made her feel safe.

I couldn't kill them. I couldn't do it, and that meant I couldn't save Destin. I let out a cry of rage that echoed through the trees and slammed my fist into the side panel of my truck.

What the hell was I supposed to do?

My wolf jumped to attention as a voice suddenly echoed in my head.

You don't have to do this alone.

My insides liquified as heat spread through me, warming my fingers and toes. I imagined Callista walking back into the clearing and finding me gone. Finding the dagger gone. I assumed she would've hated me. Just like my pack, she would've seen my weakness and abandoned me to my fate.

But Destin hadn't abandoned me. Bill had welcomed me in with open arms. And Callista...

Maybe your wolf is trying to teach you something.

I wiped my lips on my sleeve and grabbed my water bottle from the cupholder in my door. After rinsing my mouth, I jumped back onto my seat, threw the truck into reverse and whipped it around, heading in the opposite direction.

I'D BEEN to Black Lake twice before. Once when I'd stalked Nathan Black and once when I'd stolen the dagger. The houses grew closer as I passed the "Welcome to Black Lake" sign, and I pushed down the nausea. Now that I knew what Nathan had done, how he'd hurt Callista, I wanted a do-over.

Rowan's house, where I'd found the dagger, was at the end of an unmarked cul-de-sac. I was almost at the turn off when I caught sight of him. He was standing outside a mechanic shop with Jasper. I turned off the road, my tires crunching the gravel until they hit concrete, and I parked.

I stared at the two men standing in the middle of the lot.

The mechanic shop had a worn wooden sign above the garage door. My skin prickled. This could go one of two ways, and I didn't want to get into a public brawl.

I pushed open my door and stepped out.

Rowan's nostrils flared, and his eyes flicked down to my hand where I clutched the dagger. "Kael."

The tension was palpable, crackling in the air like static electricity. Rowan's nostrils flared as he shifted his weight. Jasper tensed, his body coiling like a spring, but a subtle shake of Rowan's head kept him in place.

I glanced around, a piece of me hoping I'd find Lana or Callista even though Lana's truck wasn't out front. I stopped a few feet from them and held up the dagger, the polished steel catching the light. "I've had a change of heart." I tossed it, and it clattered onto the concrete between us.

The autumn breeze rustled the leaves on the trees, and I breathed in the faint tang of oil and metal from the shop. When Rowan didn't speak, I continued. "A friend of mine is convinced the Shadow Pack is returning. I saw proof. In Lana."

Rowan considered this. "How is that supposed to help us? If the Alliance is after our packs—"

"How do you know that?" My jaw tensed.

"Callista." Rowan folded his arms in front of him. "She told me I shouldn't blame you for taking the dagger. That they're holding a friend of yours."

My chest tightened. "I don't know anything that can help you. But I can't do what they've asked." I turned and started back toward my truck.

"Kael."

I stopped at Rowan's bark.

"Your friend. The one taken by the alphas. Callista wants to get a group together to find him."

I turned, frowning. "No. The Alliance is powerful—"

"But that's what you're planning, isn't it?" Rowan walked toward me. I didn't answer him, but he knew he'd hit money.

Rowan stopped in front of me. "I'm sorry about Bill, Kael."

The words felt like a punch in the gut. I nodded once. I didn't want to talk about this, but the words slipped out anyway. "Is Callista okay?"

Rowan's jaw worked. "No."

My stomach twisted. "What happened?"

"What the hell do you think happened? She's safe, but she's not okay."

My heart started to race. I tried to turn, but Rowan put a hand on my shoulder. He stood on the concrete, which put us at eye level. "We're working on building our own alliance. I know you're not a fan of packs—"

"I'm fine on my own."

Rowan nodded once. "Yeah. I'm aware." He dropped his arm and took a step back. "But maybe a pack needs you."

THIRTY-TWO

Callista

Lana drove, her hand resting on the gear shift. I sat in the passenger seat, still buzzing with adrenaline and exhaustion. I glanced down at the torn upholstery. The leather was shredded, claw marks raking across the dashboard, and tufts of fur were scattered between the seats. I turned to look back at Evelyn and noticed a piece of my coat stuck to the seatbelt. She smiled at me, her eyes filled with tears.

She reached out and touched my arm. "Why didn't you tell me?" she mouthed, and I shrugged. What was there to say? She grabbed my hand and held it tightly as she leaned forward.

"I'm so glad you're okay," she whispered, and I nodded, my throat too tight to speak.

As we drove, I couldn't help but think about the chaos of

the meeting. The disbelief on everyone's faces when Lana and I spilled everything.

I was grateful for Evelyn's presence. For the way she'd walked into the room with me, her hand in mine.

Lana's eyes flicked to the two of us. She smirked. "Think we should stop for a milkshake?"

We pulled into the parking lot of Burger Blast, the neon sign flickering against the night sky. It was the only place in town open past eleven and it showed. The parking lot was packed.

Lana grabbed the keys from the ignition, and Evelyn and I slid out the passenger side. We walked in and found the last open booth in the back by the washrooms. The vinyl seats were cracked, and a waitress with greying hair and a name tag that read "Bill" shuffled over to take our order.

My stomach clenched.

Evelyn grinned. "Is that your real name or did you steal someone else's pin?"

Lana met my eyes.

"My name won't fit on the tag, so I took an old one." The waitress didn't even look up from her order pad. "What can I get you?"

We ordered our milkshakes, then sank into the seats.

"Well, that meeting was something." I drew a deep breath, trying to think of anything other than the dagger protruding from Bill's chest.

Lana scoffed. "I've seen less chaos at a Black Lake initiation ceremony."

"Kootenay," Evelyn corrected. "If we don't even use the new pack name, we can't expect everyone else to."

I raised an eyebrow. "You do initiations?"

Evelyn smirked. "Don't worry, nobody's going to ask Kitimat to walk over hot coals or anything. Yet."

It was funny, but I couldn't laugh. Instead, I let out a long breath, turning to look out the window. "I can't believe Lyra was there." The witch hadn't been surprised at all to hear about how the Alliance was trying to use the dagger. She had to know more than she'd given Rowan and Evelyn when they'd talked with her last.

Lana's expression turned serious. "I know. That was a shock."

I traced a crack in the vinyl with my finger. "Do you think the prophecy is real?"

Evelyn sighed. "Lyra seems to think it is."

Lana's eyes dropped. I didn't need to ask what she believed. She'd seen proof of the Shadow Pack. It wasn't a stretch to believe the rest of the legends.

Evelyn tapped her fingers on the table. "If the dagger's here, the rest of the relics could be out there somewhere, too. What if we're already too late?"

"That's why we're warning the other packs, right?" Lana looked back to the counter. She was antsy.

I smiled at Evelyn. "Rowan did well. Starting to build the alliance here. Now that we have Tori and Mara, it won't be long before the other packs join us."

Evelyn nodded. "But the alpha Alliance up north...I don't know." Her lips twitched.

The waitress with the stolen name tag brought out our milkshakes, and I took a long sip, the cold sweetness washing over my tongue.

Lana licked whipped cream from her lips. "We have to find a way to challenge them. They're not invincible."

"But they have the dagger," I muttered. And Kael. My heart felt like it was in a vacuum-sealed bag.

Evelyn frowned. "No they don't."

I stared at the swirl of vanilla in my glass. "Kael took it.

When Lana and I came back to the clearing—"

"No, he didn't." Evelyn pulled her phone from her pocket. She scrolled, then turned her screen to face us. "Rowan has it."

I blinked and read the message. Rowan had texted saying he would be late because he needed to store the dagger. *Was he talking about the same one?* "That's not possible."

Evelyn shrugged and set her phone on the seat. "You can call him yourself if you want." She slid out of the booth. "I'll be right back. I have to use the washroom."

Lana leaned in the second she was gone. "Kael took the dagger."

"I know."

"So if Rowan has it—"

"Stop, Lana." I clenched my hand around my milkshake glass. I needed to think. Why would Kael take the dagger to Rowan? Why wouldn't he tell us? Wait for us? My wolf had pushed a message to his, and I'd heard nothing back.

"Thank you, by the way." Lana's voice was low.

I looked up. "For what?"

"For not telling Rowan."

She didn't have to say anything else. Rowan had heard Bill talk about the legends. He may have his suspicions, but he didn't see what had happened at the pools. Lana had been quiet the whole drive. I had no idea what was swirling through her head. Especially after what Bill had said to her as he died.

I leaned forward, taking another sip and using my straw to mix the ice cream into the milk. "I figured you had a reason."

Lana nodded.

When Evelyn returned, we finished our milkshakes, paid, and went back to the truck.

The drive back to the house was quiet, the only sound the hum of the engine and the crunch of gravel under the tires. The excitement from the meeting had faded, and all three of us had sunk back into our own thoughts. Our own worries.

I stared out the window, wondering where Kael was at that moment. My ribs felt too tight for my lungs.

Had he brought the dagger back?

I was simultaneously relieved and broken by that news. Yes, the dagger was safe. But that meant he hadn't left the clearing to fulfill his contract. He hadn't left me behind to protect his friend.

He'd left because he didn't want a mate.

He'd left because he didn't want *me*.

I thanked Lana and Evelyn as I dropped from the truck and stalked up my drive.

My home. It felt like an eternity since I'd been here. The house was quiet as I walked in, and I dropped my things in the entryway and took off my boots.

My bedroom door creaked as I pushed it open, and I stepped inside, closing it behind me. I sat on the edge of my bed, staring at the pile of work files on my nightstand. One weekend. I hadn't even missed any work.

I nearly laughed out loud. I couldn't even imagine going back to the office and pretending like the weekend had never happened. It was like I'd changed three sizes and was trying to put on my old clothes.

Nothing fit.

How could I go back to this? How could I sit in meetings? Sit in front of my computer? Make dinner or sit around and talk with Celeste and Blake?

I stood and walked to the window, pulling open the pane and resting my hands on the sill. The forest was a dark silhouette against the indigo sky, the moonlight casting long shadows that danced with the swaying branches. I closed my eyes and leaned forward, letting the cool air wash over me.

How? How could he just leave? I'd seen the good in him. Felt it. I'd seen the way he looked at me, the way he fought to protect me. And then he'd just...walked away.

All the work I'd done to keep myself whole that evening crumbled. I broke. Tears streamed down my cheeks as I turned and slumped to the floor, dropping my head to my knees.

I couldn't do this. I didn't want to do this.

I allowed myself a few more minutes in my pity party, then started to undress, pulling my shirt over my head and tossing it onto the chair in the corner of the room. As I reached for the button on my jeans, I heard a noise outside. *Had I closed the window?*

I froze, my fingers hovering over the waistband. It was probably just the wind, or maybe a deer. But something inside me was on high alert. I crept back to the window and peered out, my eyes scanning the darkness.

Nothing.

I let out a breath and turned back to the room, but then I heard it again. A rustling. Closer this time. My heart leapt into my throat, and I stepped back, my pulse pounding in my ears.

It was probably nothing, but after the weekend I'd had, I couldn't be too sure. I held my breath, listening intently.

Then, without warning, a voice echoed in my mind.

I need you this time.

THIRTY-THREE

KAEL

I stood outside her window. I'd driven out of town and come back twice before finally going to the address Rowan gave me. My hair was mussed, my eyes bleary from lack of sleep, but once I'd made the decision, I couldn't wait a second longer to see her.

My wolf prowled. Finally he and I were both on the same page, but ironically, that didn't matter much. Callista had the final say in whether we got it.

I hadn't been able to stop thinking about her since I'd left her in the woods, and now that I was standing here, I wasn't sure what I'd been expecting. That she would be grateful? That she would throw her arms around me and tell me I was absolved of all the pain my actions had caused?

Callista didn't move. She was in a bra and jeans, and my

eyes tracked over her skin. I wanted to touch her, wanted to taste her. My hand started to shake.

She pressed her hands into the sill. "Why did you run?"

She knew I'd taken the dagger and left. Since she and Lana hadn't been at the garage, I doubted she knew I'd changed my mind and returned the relic to Rowan. None of that made her question easy to answer. "I was afraid."

Her lip twitched. "You kill people for a living."

"So people keep reminding me."

She didn't blink. "I have a hard time believing Lana or I had you shaking in your boots."

I chuckled darkly. "You've had me shaking in my boots since the first moment I saw you in your tent." I took a step closer to the window. "It's never been easy to do what I do, but it was manageable. On my own, I could compartmentalize my life. It wasn't who I was, it was what I did. To survive. Always to survive." I took another step. "The problem is...it doesn't seem manageable anymore."

"Why not?" Callista's eyes shone. Her wolf was close to the surface, pushing toward mine.

I'd already laid my life out for her at the river, so I didn't understand why it was so hard to say it this time. My tongue felt thick. My throat dry. "I have nothing to offer. I—"

"I didn't ask what you have to offer. I asked why your life isn't manageable anymore."

I struggled to hold back the tidal wave of arguments that screamed at me to run back into the trees. To get as far from Black Lake as possible because I couldn't handle it if she turned me away. I'd survived the rejection of my pack, but I couldn't survive a rejection from her.

I swallowed my fear. "Because I didn't need anything before."

"And now?"

"I need you," I rasped. My body felt like it was going to cleave in two as I searched her face for any sign that she didn't hate what she was hearing.

Callista's lips pursed. "You've known me for three days, Kael. Three days of me being terrified and in pain. That's not who I am—"

"If that's who you are at your worst, then I can't imagine the best." I strode forward until I had to crane my neck to meet her eyes. "You're curious. Calm under pressure. Smart and willing to get your hands dirty." A lump formed in my throat. "You see me."

Her cool facade cracked at that. She drew a breath and exhaled. "Inside."

"What?"

"I don't want to have this conversation through a window. Can you come inside, please?"

My heart thumped in my chest. I reached up for the sill, and Callista swatted my hand. "Lana isn't sleeping in the hall. You can come in the front door."

I nodded once, then jogged to the front of the house. I scanned for a vehicle but only saw a car that I assumed was hers. Callista pushed the door open as I took the steps two at a time.

As soon as I was next to her in the entryway, I couldn't keep from touching her. I dragged my hand over her arm, and she smiled.

"Not here. Blake will be back soon. Just take off your boots."

My blood heated. "Giving orders again?"

Callista's cheeks flushed. I set my boots next to hers and followed her down the hall to her room. She walked in and closed the window, then drew the shades.

I shut the door behind me.

Callista turned to face me. "I thought you took the dagger to complete your assignment. To save your friend."

I ran a hand through my hair, trying to tame it. "I was never going to complete my assignment. I knew that before we went to Swan Lake or I wouldn't have gone."

"Because of what we tried to do with the dagger?"

I nodded. "I thought about taking it back to the alphas."

"But you gave it to Rowan." Callista took a few steps toward me, and the walls of her room suddenly seemed to press in on me.

"He told me about your plan." I moved toward her, and we met at the foot of her bed.

Her eyebrow quirked. "Which one?"

"To put together a rescue group." I slid my arm around her waist and pulled her closer. "You didn't know I was coming back with the dagger."

Callista arched against me. "It didn't matter."

"Didn't it?"

She shook her head. "They might have others. We need to show them they can't harm our packs or other shifters to cow us into submission."

I brushed my lips over her forehead. "So it wasn't just for me?"

She pressed a hand to my cheek, and the corner of her mouth lifted. "Definitely not."

I leaned into her touch. "I need to say it now. All the things I don't have to offer you."

Callista laughed, dropping her hand to my shoulder. "You've already told me how inadequate you are."

I fixed my eyes on her. "I'm serious, Callista."

She smiled up at me, her eyes glassy. "I know you are. I'm just waiting for you to realize that I don't care where you came from or what you've done."

"Callista—"

"And it's not because I haven't thought about it. I have. The moment I felt a pull toward you, I listed every reason why it would be a terrible idea. But then I walked back into this empty room and envisioned stepping back into my old life…"

I ran my hands over her healed skin. "It would be different. You wouldn't be in pain."

She shook her head. "Yes I would." Callista pushed up on her tip toes and kissed the underside of my jaw. "You're right. We've seen each other at our worst. Maybe that's a gift."

My head was thick, the scent of her hijacking my rational mind. "How could it be a gift?"

She pressed her hand against the base of my throat. "We have nothing to hide from each other."

I worked to catch my breath. "I can't give you promises. I don't know what my life will look like—who I'll be."

Callista nodded, but she didn't back away. "I don't need promises, Kael. I only need one."

THIRTY-FOUR

CALLISTA

B lake's truck sounded in the drive and we stood there silent, staring at each other. My wolf paced, ready to leap out of my skin. She needed him the way plants needed water. It was primal. Carnal. Spiritual. The thrill of it sent shivers down my spine.

The front door opened. "Callista?"

"Yeah!" I called out, never breaking my gaze.

Blake tromped down the hall. "Are you okay?"

"Mmhmm. Just going to bed."

Blake shuffled his weight, and the floorboards creaked. "There's an extra set of boots at the front door. I—"

"They're mine, Blake."

He was silent a moment. "They're huge."

Kael raised an eyebrow, and I stifled a laugh. "Yep. A friend of mine left them in Lana's truck."

"Got it." Blake sighed. "Do you need anything?"

"Go to sleep, Blake."

He walked back down the hall. "Goodnight."

"'Night."

Kael waited until he heard dishes clattering in the sink before lifting me off the floor and throwing me on the bed.

"Shh!" I laughed, but Kael's hand was already at the waistband of my jeans.

"Off," he whispered. He flicked open the button, and I yanked them over my hips. He pulled them off and threw them on the floor.

Kael stripped off his shirt and lay down next to me, pulling me against him. My body responded like a magnet, pressing against the hard planes of his chest. I wanted to drown in his scent as he lowered his head and pressed his lips against the nape of my neck.

His lips were everywhere. Dragging over my collarbone, my jaw, then finally over my mouth. He tasted of mint as his tongue teased mine, and I moaned. His grip on my hips tightened as he rolled his hips against mine.

The urge to tear off his clothes, to feel his bare skin against mine warred with my desire to savor every second. I let my hands wander, exploring the muscles of his back as he moved against me.

Kael's hands slid under my shirt, his fingers grazing the sensitive skin just below my ribs. I arched into him, and he groaned. His breath was hot against my ear as he whispered, "I need you."

I nodded, unable to form words. My body was a live wire, every nerve ending on high alert. Kael's hand moved lower, slipping under the waistband of my underwear, and I gasped. He and I both knew this wasn't like last time. This wasn't release. This was what our wolves had known we needed all along.

A physical and spiritual bond. A melding of our souls and our magic.

"Your my mate," I whispered. "I want you as my mate."

"I'm yours," he growled.

His damn fingers worked me into a frenzy, and I teetered on the edge, on the brink of oblivion. I grasped his hand and opened my eyes, my breath coming in ragged gasps. Kael's eyes were dark, his pupils dilated. He looked like a man possessed, and I was his willing victim.

"I can't do this again," I whispered, and as his face fell, realized he hadn't understood. I wrapped my hand around his neck and pulled him closer. "When I bond with you, I can't be quiet. I'm already going to bite right through my tongue."

Kael let out a shaky breath. "I thought you meant—"

"I know. Poor choice of words. I'm sorry."

He pulled back and met my eyes, the wheels in his head turning. Then he slid off the bed and motioned for me to stand. When I did, he grabbed the quilt off my bed and yanked open the window.

"Kael, what are you doing?" I whispered, but he didn't answer. Instead, he threw the quilt out onto the grass and jumped after it.

I stood there for a split second, dumbfounded, then ran to the window. The night air was cool against my flushed skin. "I'm not going to jump!" I hissed.

Kael reached up, his eyes dancing. "Just sit on the sill. I'll pull you out." I did as he asked, supporting myself as Kael grasped my lower half.

When my feet touched the grass, I laughed. "This feels naughty."

Kael grinned. "I thought you'd like it." He threw the quilt at me, then crouched and motioned for me to get on his back.

I laughed and climbed on. "What, no harness this time?"

Kael bucked playfully as he stood, then took off with only socks on his feet into the trees.

"Do you know where you're going?" I asked.

Kael grunted. "Far enough that Blake won't hear you scream."

My stomach dropped like I'd just hit the highest point on a playground swing and was plummeting back to the earth. "You've never heard me scream."

"I'm looking forward to it."

Kael carried me five more minutes then stopped when we reached a break in the trees. He panted as I spread the quilt out on the ground, then turned to face him. The moonlight filtered through the branches, casting a soft glow on his face.

I took a step forward, and he closed the distance between us. His hands were on me again, and I melted into his touch. The knowledge that there was no rush, no need to hold back, sent electricity flaring through me.

Kael's hand roamed my body, exploring every curve and hollow. He unclasped my bra, finding new skin to suck and tease.

My hands fumbled with the buttons on his jeans, and Kael helped me, pulling them off and tossing them to the side. His skin was warm under my hands, his muscles taut and ready. I ran my fingers over his chest, then tentatively explored his second arm. The one that never fully formed.

Kael sucked air through his teeth.

"I'm sorry, does it hurt?"

He shook his head. "No, I—nobody ever touches me there. It's...sensitive." His eyes were closed, and his skin prickled under my touch.

"I want to touch you there." I watched his face as I pressed my lips to his skin, kissing my way over his shoulder and down, holding his arm in my hands. "You're shaking."

"This is terrifying."

I frowned, nipping at him. "Why?"

He clenched his jaw. "Showing you my weakness. Letting you see all of me."

I straightened, cupping his face in my hands. "I don't see any weakness. I love every part of you. Maybe that part best."

Kael huffed a laugh. "Best?"

I grinned. "Second best?"

Kael slipped my underwear off, and I stood before him, completely exposed. I didn't feel an ounce of self-consciousness. *Safe.*

"Callista," he growled, and my wolf howled inside me. I reached out. Kael grabbed my hands, pulling me down onto the quilt with him.

He positioned himself over me, his body a cage of heat and muscle. Kael lowered himself, his lips brushing against my ear. "I want to hear you say it," he whispered, and his breath sent shivers down my spine.

"I want you, Kael. You're mine. My mate." My voice was barely a whisper, but it was enough.

Kael's eyes darkened, and I gasped as our bodies melded into one. We moved in perfect sync, both of us reading the other like braille. I clung to him, my nails digging into his back, as color and heat swirled within me.

My wolf was wild, her energy crackling like electricity. She wanted to claim him, to mark him as ours. My heartbeat quickened, and I knew Kael could hear it. Could feel my pulse under his fingertips.

"I'll take care of you. I'll protect you, always." His voice was rough as he sank his teeth into my shoulder, marking me his.

A wave of euphoria pulsed through me as our magic, our wolves connected, swirling into one. I returned the mark, biting the side of his neck with his pulse hot against my tongue.

"Kael—" I threw my head back, my body exploding in pleasure as I cried out into the night. Wave after wave crashed over me, my body convulsing with the intensity of it. Kael's grip on my hips tightened. He tensed above me, and then collapsed, his body slick with sweat.

For a moment, the world was silent except for the sound of our breathing. I gripped him, reveling in the weight of him before he rolled off me, pulling me into his arms. The night air was cool against my skin, but his body was a furnace, keeping me warm.

We lay there in silence, our bodies entwined. The steady beat of Kael's heart against my back was the most comforting sensation in the world.

Finally, Kael spoke. "Well, that was a first."

I laughed, the sound muffled against his chest. "What, you don't usually drag women off into the woods?"

Kael's chest rumbled with laughter. "Not usually, no."

I turned in his arms, my head resting on his shoulder. "Thank you," I whispered.

Kael's brow furrowed. "For what?"

"For making it perfect." I reached up, tracing the lines of his jaw with my fingers. "For making me feel wanted." We lay on the quilt, limbs tangled together, and stared up at the stars.

"I think your wolf is finally satisfied," he murmured, his voice a low rumble in his chest.

I raised my head and grinned. "She's been very patient, I'll have you know."

Kael chuckled. "Patient? That's not the word I would've used."

I kissed his shoulder, my skin buzzing. "Alphas. Always so stubborn." I pushed up on my elbows. "You realize you do have a pack now."

He raised an eyebrow. "A pack of two?"

I nodded. "I'll follow you anywhere, Kael."

He brushed a tendril of hair from my cheek. "What if I lead you astray?"

I turned my cheek into the palm of his hand. "Oh. I'm counting on it."

EPILOGUE

LANA

I paced back and forth in my room, unable to find a moment of peace. The door was locked, and I couldn't help but glance out the window at the lush northern forest that surrounded the small town of Black Lake. The redwood trees stood tall and silent, a stark contrast to the turmoil raging inside me.

I couldn't stay here. I knew that.

I'd gotten the messages from Rowan and Jasper. The dagger was safe. Locked up. It should have been enough.

But it wasn't.

I felt like something was pulling me, tethering me to something I couldn't see. I couldn't explain it, but I knew it had everything to do with the dagger. The relic.

A sudden knock at the door made me jump. I quickly

composed myself, trying to mask the storm inside as I opened it.

Rowan stood there, his eyes searching mine. "Lana, are you okay?"

I forced a smile. "Yeah, I'm fine. Just a bit restless, I guess." My answer was superficial, and we both knew it.

Rowan didn't buy it. "Lana, I need to know what's going on."

I swallowed hard, then turned, pretending to straighten my coat hanging on the hooks. "I heard the dagger is safe."

He nodded. "Not convinced?"

I opened my mouth to argue, but the words caught in my throat. I couldn't keep up the charade any longer. "I don't know, Rowan. Something about it . . . I can't explain."

Rowan's expression softened. "You don't have to explain. Just tell me what you need." His voice was gentle, a stark contrast to the commanding tone he usually used.

I hesitated, then shook my head. "I don't know what I need. I just feel like . . . like I'm being pulled in a million different directions, and I can't control it."

Rowan reached out and took my hand, his touch grounding me. "Lana, you don't have to do this alone. You have the pack. You have me."

My heart ached at his words. I wanted to believe him, but the truth was, I didn't feel like I belonged anywhere. Not with the pack, not with myself. "I'm not sure about that."

Rowan studied me for a moment, then reached into his pocket and pulled out the dagger. My eyes widened, and I stepped back.

"I know what you are, Lana." His voice was calm.

I swallowed hard. "Rowan, I—"

He held up a hand. "You don't have to explain. I understand

more than you think." He placed the dagger in my hand, and I gasped as the contact sent a jolt of energy through me.

"How did you—"

Rowan stepped back. "I don't need you to explain, Lana. I know about the Shadow Pack."

My heart pounded in my chest. "Rowan, I can't—"

He shook his head. "Lana, I've already talked to Blake. He's ready to step in as my third. You can go."

My breath caught in my throat. "What?"

Rowan's eyes softened. "You don't have to stay, Lana. I'm not going to hold you to that. You can do what you need to do."

Tears pricked at the corners of my eyes. He was giving me an out, and I didn't know whether to be grateful or devastated. I nodded, unable to find the words to express the whirlwind of emotions inside me. Instead, I stepped forward and wrapped my arms around him, holding on for a moment longer than I should have.

When I finally pulled away, Rowan looked at me with an intensity that made my knees weak. "Thank you, Lana. For everything."

I opened my mouth to respond, but the words caught in my throat. He turned and walked down the steps. I watched until he pulled out of the driveway, then snatched my jacket from the hooks and slid on my shoes.

I wasn't sure what I was going to do, but one thing was clear: I couldn't stay in Black Lake.

It was late. I walked quickly, nearly jogging as I got to Callista's drive.

The light in her room was on. I knocked softly on the door, but there was no answer. I tried the handle, but it was locked. Frustration bubbled up inside me as I ran around the side of the house and found her window at the back.

It was open. "Callista?"

"Lana?" Callista squeaked.

There was a thump, then two very guilty faces peered over the sill.

Why wasn't I the least bit surprised? I held out the dagger. "If you want to get dressed, I have a proposition you might be interested in."

Buy Book #3 in the series

ABOUT THE AUTHOR

Luna masquerades as a well-adjusted, functioning adult, but she secretly still believes in magic and wild things hidden just beyond the veil of our world. She has a fairy garden (with lights!) and lives with her husband and children near the Rocky Mountains in Colorado. She adores shiny objects.

www.ingramcontent.com/pod-product-compliance
Lightning Source LLC
Chambersburg PA
CBHW032222190726
48289CB00007BA/2348